Harold Fielding-Hall

Thibaw's Queen

Harold Fielding-Hall

Thibaw's Queen

ISBN/EAN: 9783337321611

Printed in Europe, USA, Canada, Australia, Japan

Cover: Foto ©Andreas Hilbeck / pixelio.de

More available books at **www.hansebooks.com**

THIBAW'S QUEEN

BY

H. FIELDING

AUTHOR OF "THE SOUL OF A PEOPLE"

ILLUSTRATED

LONDON AND NEW YORK
HARPER & BROTHERS
45 ALBEMARLE STREET, W.
1899

CONTENTS

CONTENTS

LIST OF ILLUSTRATIONS

vii

THIBAW'S QUEEN

CHAPTER I

THE BURMESE

THE immemorial East has passed into a proverb. To us new nations of the west Asia is a country of the past. We think of it as the land where the empires of Babylon and Assyria, of Persia and India, of China and Japan flourished long ago. For two thousand years Asia stood in the vanguard of progress. When we were savages colouring ourselves with woad, and clothing ourselves with skins the east gloried in an old civilisation. Great conquerors lived and fought and erected kingdoms and founded cities. Great rulers arose and made laws and consolidated these kingdoms, and welded the peoples into a whole. Great prophets were born whose teachings spread throughout the earth.

Science was cultivated there and prospered, art rose and became very glorious, and there was a beautiful literature. But all that was long ago.

The empires of Assyria and Babylon, where are they? India has fallen beneath our feet, and become our vassal. How has the strength of China departed! The great warriors and their spirit have all gone, leaving but a memory. And the cities that they founded are become dust. Asia is a land of forgotten cities. The mud which the peasant of to-day kneads into bricks for his hut is crumbled from the walls of palaces.

Everywhere you go you pass over the graves of dead dynasties.

The religions, too, that were great in those days do not fit the changed world; the great faiths that once arose and spread so fast are become lifeless.

The art has gone utterly. Who could now build the temples of Humpi or design the Taj?

And the people seem to us to have become moribund. Centuries ago they were full of life and invention. Now they lie bound in old tradition and beliefs, outworn rags of garments that once were useful. The minds of the people of Asia seem to us, much as their country is, crowded with the ruins of the glories of other days, so that there is hardly any room for new things.

We have come to look upon the whole East in this light. To say that anything is eastern is to say that if it be old it is good, if modern it is bad. An eastern land must be a land whose only and great attraction is in its relics and its memories of the past. An eastern people must by the very nature of things be a very old nation, once strong and civilised and young, now old and feeble, falling back into chaos.

The very word "asiatic" expresses all these things, they are inherent in its meaning we think. And yet this is not entirely true.

There are old countries and old nations in Asia, yet all Asia is not old, nor are all orientals the mere survivals of great peoples. There are in Asia very young peoples, as young as the youngest of European nations, as innocent of a great past as any people can be, as unbound of tradition as a child is.

In the valley of the great Irrawaddy, shut off on either hand by great mountain walls from the old-world empires of India and of China, there lives a people that is younger than any western people.

In Burma there is no immemorial past, there is hardly any past at all, any history save of legend and of story. Whereas in India and China there were empires two thousand years ago, in Burma it is not yet one hundred and fifty years since Alompra welded the different tribes into one people. Before then the history of Burma is merely that of warring clans, of many little kingdoms, as of England in the Heptarchy and before. A strong man would arise and conquer the surrounding countries and found a little city, his dynasty would endure for a time and die out. All over Burma there are the ruins of the capitals of such tiny kingdoms, none of them very old. Indeed Burma is such a very new country that it is very hard to find buildings of any antiquity. With the exception of the pagodas at Pagan, which are eight hundred years old or so, and a few ruins buried in the jungles, there is nothing in the country that is not of to-day; even the Shwe Dagon Pagoda is not four hundred years old. You may travel all over Burma and hardly find a pagoda or an edifice of any kind that speaks to you of the past.

Mandalay, the royal city, was only founded in 1859, not forty years ago. And as with its history and its buildings so it is with its art and its learning. Whatever art you find that is worth admiring, whatever knowledge of any kind you may discover, it is of to-day. The wood carving and silver work is new within the last hundred years. It is only within the last fifty that they have risen to any great beauty. There is more art in the workers of to-day than of any time. No Burman graver or carver can look back with regret to other days. These arts have sprung out of nothing within the memory of men still living.

As it is with the land and with the art so it is with the people. The Burmans are not as we imagine all orientals to be. They are bound by no traditions of the past. They have no objection to new things, but take to them readily when they understand their value. They have no caste to drag them back and hamper them in the race of life. They have no traditions of a great past to live down to.

Whereas in India it is common to hear people speak of the great days of three and four hundred years ago, in Burma I never heard any one talk except of King Mindon's time. His was a golden reign they say, and he died in 1878.

They are a modern people, an infant people in every possible meaning of the word. Whatever of them is best worth learning is comprised within the last two reigns, of King Mindon and his son King Thibaw. And yet of the events of these two reigns, events that took place within the past forty years, it is extraordinary to find how ignorant we are, how little we actually know of the kings and of the government of those times. If they had been a thousand years ago we could not know less. We have a few curious stories and that is all.

But the reasons are not far to seek. One reason is that perhaps we have not thought the history of these things would be worth learning. We have come to Burma classing it in our minds with the rest of the East. We have assumed that the Burmans too are the outworn remains of a great people, and that whatever period of their history may be worth learning must be long ago and cannot be a recent one. And so although attempts have been made to decipher the monuments of past reigns, to disinter bricks and read their legends, and tell again the stories that we find on them, no one has cared to inquire into the reigns of the last two kings of Burma. They are too recent for us to care about them.

As regards the history of King Thibaw another reason is probably here. In later years the Burmese government of independent Burma and the government of India were not on good terms. There was always suspicion and doubt between them. The Burmese remembered the two wars of 1825 and 1852, when they were defeated and lost their best provinces. There was the bitterness of defeat. And they thought that we

were not yet content, that we had only refrained
from annexing the whole country because at the
time it was too big a mouthful for us, and that we
only sought a good opportunity to complete what
our former wars had begun.

This intensified the natural concealment and
reticence of an oriental government. Looking
upon us as foes, they did not care in any way to
justify and explain to us their acts. Expecting us
to wilfully misunderstand them and find evil where
we could, the Burmese government and people saw
no use in trying to make matters plain and put
their conduct in a fair and clear light. Explana-
tions would be a weakness, and moreover useless
to an enemy determined to see only the worst.

Therefore in place of the authoritative statements
of those who knew, the news that reached our
agents and our papers was usually merely the tales
of spies whose only concern was to speak evilly.

An autocratic government, like any other, must
make enemies. A king and queen in the position
of King Thibaw and Queen Supayalat must make
many enemies. And it was from these enemies
that the reports that reached us of the doings of the
king and of the government arose. Friends of the
palace and of the people kept their own counsel
afar from the foreigners; enemies were only too

ready to pour their grievances and scandals into our, as they hoped, sympathetic ears, hoping thereby to obtain vengeance upon those who had injured them. These reports were generally believed.

I do not think we are a very kindly people. We are generally glad, I think, to hear evil of other people and believe it. It suits with our ideas of the eternal fitness of things that other nations and governments should be wicked. More especially when the other people have, we know, a feeling of hatred and of bitterness towards ourselves.

So partly through our own fault, partly through the fault of the Burmese themselves, the only stories that obtained credence and circulation about the king and his people were to their discredit. It was in this way that arose the tales of the continual drunkenness of the king, of the blood-thirstiness of the queen, of the utter wickedness of the palace in general. Little sparks of truth were fanned into huge flares that lit the whole history of these years with lurid light. Tale-teller vied with tale-teller as to which could impute most wickedness to the palace, regardless of truth or even of prob-ability. Yet consider how improbable those tales were, how impossible of belief to any one who stayed for a moment to consider them!

The king was a confirmed drunkard. Yet every

one knows that Buddhists are total abstainers, and allow no liquor to be manufactured or opium imported into the country. Every one also who cared to know could learn that King Thibaw was a very rigid Buddhist, was famed as a learned monk before he came to the throne, was assisted and encouraged by the head of the monkhood, a man universally respected for his holiness.

And the queen was bloodthirsty. Then was she very different from the women of her nation. Who that knows them would impute ferocity to the soft-mannered, gentle-hearted women that all of us honour? The king greatly loved her and she greatly loved him. Can a wild beast such as she was represented to be love and be loved?

As I got to know the people I became sure that these tales could not be true, and gradually the curiosity came to me to try and find out what had really given rise to them. Such a search could not but be interesting. For life in the palace in Mandalay was not like life anywhere in the west nowadays. It seemed from all that I could hear that it would be more like looking a thousand years back into the days of the charmed Bagdad, than hearing a tale of yesterday. The whole atmosphere was full of hidden loves and secret murders, of plots and counter-plots, of passion and of colour, such as we know not now. It was a new Arabian night's tale this tale of the palace of Mandalay, only greater and better. Behind these stories that were exciting and false I thought I might discover facts that would be true, and as much more exciting than the stories, as truth always is than fiction.

I tried, and I think I have succeeded. But how difficult the search has been, no one who has not tried can tell. From Englishmen it is, as I have explained, hopeless to look for the true story of those years. And from Burmese it is not much easier. To the ordinary townsman or villager, the king and the palace were as unknown as they were to us. From them nothing could be obtained. And those who did know were unwilling to tell. Fallen ministers of a fallen king were loth to tell what they knew of events in which they had themselves taken part. They regarded inquiries with distrust, and kept their knowledge to themselves. Even sometimes when they could be induced to talk it was evident that their account was onesided and was made for a foreign ear. The Burmese have not yet learnt to make books. There are no reminiscences of that reign, the last reign of the Burmese kings, there are no voluminous letters, no official memoranda, no newspaper reports. And so when it first occurred to me, that I would like to try and know something of the truth, I found all my attempts came to nothing, all sources of information were dried up.

At last a chance came.

She was a maid of honour. She had been maid of honour to the queen for four years up to the last moment of the surrender. She had lived in the palace through many of these events of which I heard such queer stories, and she had seen much that I wanted to know. It is true that she had been but a child then. She was only thirteen when Mandalay was taken. She saw but with childish eyes, heard but with childish ears. But what she had seen or heard she was willing to tell me, and I was very willing to hear. For much of it was very strange, very different to what I had heard before, very tragical it seemed to me, very beautiful.

What she told me gave me the key as to what it was that I should search for. With her account in my memory I found it much easier to draw from others that which I required to know. I found information here and missing links in the story there. And still as I have gone on I have found that her stories were true, her view of what she had seen likely to be the right one. It is strange to tell the story of a reign from information derived mostly from a girl, a maid of honour. But what could be done? Children are very candid chroniclers, they do not criticise, they do not think a thing is so because it ought to be; they see and hear, and they tell what they have known.

So far as my maid of honour's own facts go I have no doubt of them. And for the rest I have done my best. Without any state papers to consult, newspapers to read, letters, diaries, reminiscences, memoranda to derive materials from, it is somewhat of a forlorn hope trying to write the tale of the last of the Burmese kings.

It will be understood that this is no history. History is I take it an account of statecraft, of laws and of wars, of how minister succeeded minister, and policy succeeded policy, of how the people were taxed and judged. But this contains little ' of such matters. Here and there, it is true, the history of the times has become so much the personal story of the king and the queen and those who lived with them in the palace that they cannot be separated. Yet my story is rather of persons than of affairs; it is of the king and of the queen, how they came to the throne and how they acted when there, of the lives and intrigues, of the vices and virtues of those around them. It is, indeed, the life of those years as seen from the social standpoint of one who lived as maid of honour with the queen. But whatever it loses in historical value, it seems to me to gain in living interest.

To my maid of honour, the queen and king and ministers were not mere figure heads through whom came orders and commands, who were rulers and officers, but they were a man and a woman, much as other men and women are, acting much as others would if placed in the same position and surroundings. The story she tells is a living story full of the deep interest which centres in the strength and weakness of humanity, full of the pathos that clings to those who have loved deeply, have hoped much, have striven hard, and who have fallen from their great estate and lost all that makes life worth living.

For the king and queen are prisoners to-day, have been prisoners for twelve years now, will be prisoners till they die.

They will return to their kingdom never again.

CHAPTER II

KING MINDON

KING MINDON, the father of King Thibaw, came to the throne in 1854. The people were angry and restless at their defeat by the Indian government, and the annexation of the delta of the Irrawaddy, and they attributed it, as was natural, greatly to the incapacity of Pagan Min, who was the then ruler. So when after the peace the king's brother Mindon rose in rebellion and arrested Pagan in his palace at Amarapura all the people rejoiced at the change. And they had reason.

Of all the kings of Burma from Alompra to Thibaw, King Mindon was the best. The empire that was left to him was, indeed, shorn from what it had been. The provinces of Arracan, of Pegu, of Tenasserim, the richest part of Burma, were lost ; and all that was left was the northern half ot the Irrawaddy valley and the Shan Plateau. In all, Upper Burma was the size of France, but much of this was not under the direct rule of the king. In the Shan states semi-independent princes reigned, whose allegiance was principally shown by payment of tribute and by giving their daughters to be wives to the king. On the west the fierce Chin clans can hardly be said to have been subdued at all.

Burma proper extended from the mountains above Bhamo on the north to the frontier of the British province on the south, about four hundred miles. The breadth from east to west varied from one hundred to one hundred and fifty miles, and through the middle flowed the Irrawaddy river. This country of Burma proper was divided into forty-nine provinces, each under a governor appointed by the king, who had power of life and death within his charge. The capital, the centre of the kingdom, was Amarapura. This was a city built upon the banks of the Irrawaddy where it makes a great bend to the west about seven hundred miles from the sea, and behind it and below it was the most fertile land of the upper province. It was not far from Ava, which had been the capital not so long ago. For it was the custom of great kings among the Burmese to each build a capital for himself. A Burmese town is built of wood and of bamboos, and the roofs are usually of thatch. To move a big community was not the serious, nay the impossible task that it would be with us. And there were many reasons for a new king to desire a change. A palace built of wood, even of the royal teak, will not last for ever. The beams will warp and the carving will lose its brilliancy and the pinnacles become shaky. If a new palace must be built it may just as well be built in a new place. There are traditions that hang about the palaces of kings that were best forgotten. New rulers liked to begin with a fresh sheet in the minds of their people.

Therefore when King Mindon came to the throne his first idea was to build a new capital and a new palace, the most beautiful that the nation had seen, to be to them a token of a new spirit that had come upon the empire. The old city was small and cramped; the new city should be great, capable of indefinite extension. The old palace was rickety and infirm; the new should be as strong and beautiful as could be made. The old rule was one of mistakes and misfortunes; the new one should be glorious and happy.

It was not necessary to move far. Four miles north of Amarapura is a wide plain lying between the river and the Shan mountains. It is fertile land, well watered by irrigation from dams and by

THE CITY WALLS

streams that come down from the hills, suited in all ways for the site of a great city. Here beside the river the land was laid out into square blocks for the merchants and the townsfolk. The roads were broad, the main ones being those leading down to the river landing-places. To each trade was alloted a quarter, and land was reserved for monasteries and pagodas.

The city itself was built three miles away from the river. The king, it is said, objected to the noise of the steamer whistles disturbing the quiet of the palace; but a better reason seems to be that he did not like the idea of his new city and his new palace being exposed to the fire of gunboats if at any time a quarrel should again arise between Burma and the Indian government.

The walls were one and a quarter mile square, built of red brick thirty feet high, crenellated, with great gateways on each of the four sides. Within, the walls were ramped with earth, and on the top were guard-houses with pinnacled roofs lacquered and gilded, wherein the soldiers watched. Without was a moat fed with water from a stream, crossed by drawbridges and covered in the season with lotus and water-lilies of all colours. The city was for the great officials, for the troops, and for the servants of the king. Traders and common folk were not allowed land therein ; it was kept as the capital, as a fort wherein resistance might be sustained for long against any enemy.

It was laid out into squares that were given to soldiers and to the ministers.

Nearly in the centre of the city was built the palace. Here was erected a masonry platform raised six feet above the ground, and upon this the palace stood. It was a very beautiful place, this palace of the king. Even now, when its royal red is faded, its gold dropping from the walls, its gardens levelled into open spaces, it is beautiful and strange, like no other building that the world has seen. In the days of its glory it was a jewel. Around about triple walls were guard-houses wherein the troops kept watch day and night. The guard-houses were red, and they had carved façades, as had the watch-towers on the walls. The great gate was in the east, and its steps were flanked with guns. Above the audience chamber rose the glittering pinnacle of the "*centre of the universe.*"

All was covered with gold, the pillars and the huge façade, and the spire, even the cannon were gilded that guarded the steps. It was a great and blinding blaze of gold. Seen from afar off the spire gleamed with the glory of a flame. Very

GUARD-HOUSE ON CITY WALLS

high was the throne room, built with magnificent teak stems as pillars, so tall that they seemed almost slender. Within was the throne, entered by little gates from behind. Behind this throne room were the other chambers of the palace; the state rooms all gilded and the others lacquered red. They were not one great building, but innumerable small ones, each with its triple roof and its carving. Between were little courtyards where there were fountains, and there were trees that showed their tender green against the glory of the gold and red.

Facing the west as the king's throne room faced the east was the queen's throne room, only less magnificent, less beautiful, less lofty than the king's. On her side were no guns, but instead there were trees and flowers and to the north and to the south the gardens where the king and queen loved to walk. Beautiful gardens they were, with little lakes and canals crossed by narrow bridges. Winding ways there were leading to tiny hills that raised their summits crowned with bamboo plumes, and there were hidden places in the trees. In the lakes there were lotus and many kinds of lilies, and the gardens were odorous with champak and jasmine. They were small and not like our gardens, but they were beautiful for all that. There were a few other buildings within the palace enclosure but not upon the platform : a monastery, a pagoda, a mint, an arsenal, and behind the gardens many houses for the servants. If you ascend Mandalay hill that lies just to the north of the city, the whole scene is before you. There is the great city with its red walls and the moat about it like a silver girdle. There is the palace gleaming with gold amid the trees of the gardens and the busy town beyond the city walls right down to the river. And you can see the shining river itself, and beyond are the pagoda-crowned hills of Sagaing.

No king ever looked on a more beautiful capital than this. In the early morning with the sunlight making the world glad about him King Mindon came to his throne. They tell you, those who saw that sight, that such a thing was never seen before. First of all came the monks, very many of them, in yellow robes, with downcast eyes walking very slowly, and behind them soldiers of the Guard. Behind the troops came the king riding upon his elephant, a blaze of gold and silver and of jewels, and after him came more troops and ministers and a great crowd of people. Amid pomp and glory, with the firing of the guns and the shouts of a great multitude of people, King Mindon came to Mandalay. Here in this new city that he had built King Mindon lived and reigned for twenty years.

He must have been a wonderful man. Everywhere you go in Burma you hear of him and of how wise he was and how great. All things went well in his time, the people tell you ; there was righteous rule and strong government, and fair taxation. Governors were kept from oppression, robbers were suppressed, religion and trade flourished. Reforms were introduced everywhere, and with success because the people were on the side of the king.

Before his time there had been no scheme of taxation. When the kings wanted money they sent demands to the governors, who extracted the required amounts from the people and paid it into the royal treasuries. The officials had no salaries. To each official was given some province, or some town or village, and he got from it what he could. He " ate it " in Burmese phrase. The merchants and traders were at the mercy of their lords, who could squeeze them as they liked. It was dangerous to be rich in those days.

King Mindon altered all this. A uniform tax was to be levied. Every householder within the kingdom was to pay ten rupees per annum to the king's treasury. And that the distribution might be fair it was enacted that each village or quarter of the town should appoint its own assessors and collect its own taxes. So if a village contained two hundred houses it had to pay two thousand rupees, and this amount it divided among its residents according to their means. A wealthy trader would pay say fifty rupees, a labourer but two rupees. It worked in those days admirably. Then out of his treasury the king paid salaries to his governors and officials and forbade all oppression. He did more, for he saw that his commands were obeyed. Then he reformed the judicial system of the country, and made it as near as he could to a civilised system, and he was careful in hearing appeals to insure that the law was administered as it should be. Unjust judges came to great disaster in his days. He built bridges, too, and dug wells and tanks and made roads. If you inquire who built that bridge or made that lake nine times out of ten you will be told it was King Mindon who did so. He gave his royal teak freely for all public purposes, for monasteries and for rest houses and for other works of necessity. He reformed his army and began a tiny navy for the river, to patrol its great waters and maintain order. He introduced coined money in place of silver bars.

It seemed almost incredible the amount that he

did for his people. And they were grateful. Never was there such a king, they say, as King Mindon. Never was there such a happy country as Upper Burma was in his days. Gold there was then in plenty. Every girl had her golden bracelets, every man his ring and buttons. Silk, too, was cheap and plentiful, and cotton was grown in quantities, and the people spun and wove it for themselves. The rains were always good and plentiful in his reign. Since then they have become more and more scanty, so that many districts have for years hovered on the verge of famine. In King Mindon's time it was never so. The rains came in due season, and the crops were plentiful, so that the taxes were hardly felt. Religion flourished, and the monks were honoured, and education spread among all ranks of the people so that no man was illiterate. It was the golden age.

Much of King Mindon's success was due no doubt to his power of selecting worthy ministers to carry out his orders. As no man himself can do very much, but must act principally through others, it is one of the most indispensable qualities of a great man that he should be able to judge men, and to gather about him those who will understand and be able to carry them out. In this quality as in others, King Mindon was not deficient.

There were two ministers to whom much of his success is said to be due, and as they lived through King Thibaw's reign and took a leading part in all that occurred then it is necessary to mention them.

They were the Taingda Mingyi and the Kinwun Mingyi, names well known through Burma, associated irrevocably with the end of the Burmese kingdom. They seem to have been very different. The Taingda Mingyi was a man cruel and vindictive, they say, very patriotic, hating the foreigner and especially the Englishman with a bitter hatred. He was a great leader of the old party, that which believed in Burma and looked with suspicion on all new introductions from without. He seems to have been narrow minded, and is not I think generally held as a wise man. But he had authority. Throughout the country his was a name that was feared and was honoured, notwithstanding many terrible faults, as a man honest to his king, to his queen, to his country. He was a man ready to face all danger, all certainty even of disaster in support of that which he thought right. He died the other day after long exile.

But the Kinwun Mingyi was, the Burmans say, far too clever for that. He was not popular, not to compare in influence amongst the people with the Taingda Mingyi, but he was a wise man,

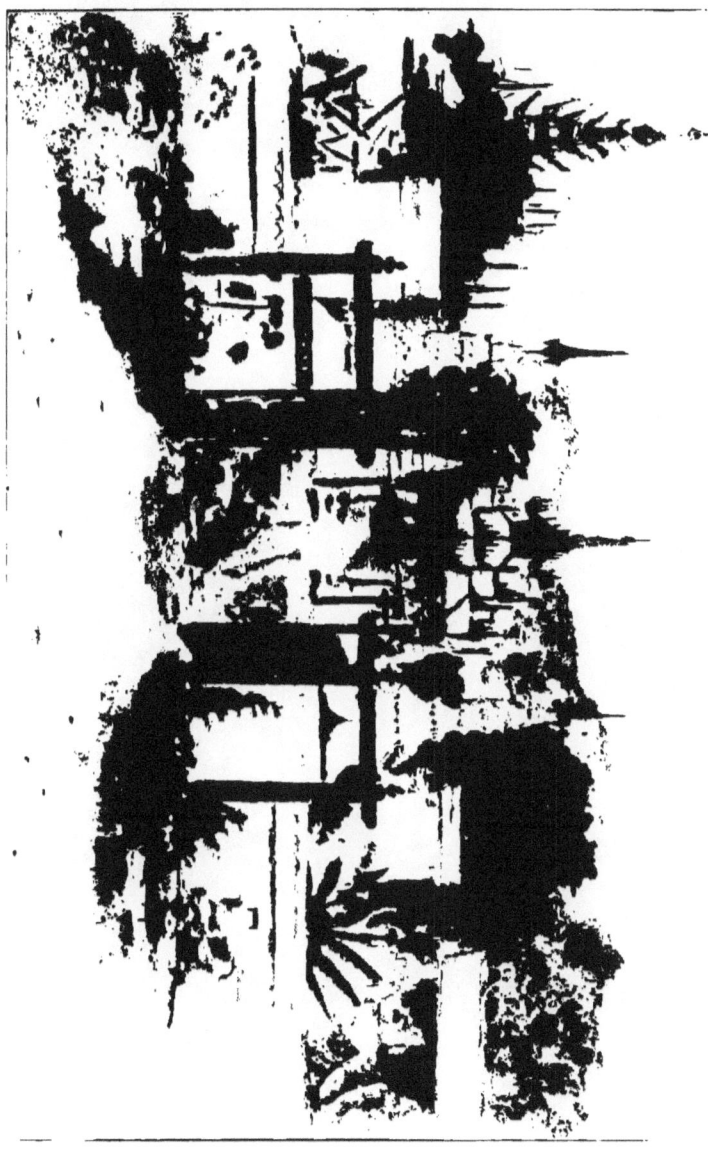

EASTERN ENTRANCE TO PALACE

seeing with clear eyes that which was coming, understanding the signs of the times, ready to make the best of circumstances for himself. And so he is alive still, decorated by the Indian government, and a recipient of a pension from them, while his king and queen are far away. The kingdom fell, but the Kinwun Mingyi remained.

Other ministers there were, but they were of small account compared with these two. No one was to be named in influence or power beside them. After King Mindon died they were left with almost supreme power for a time, until a new influence arose which overshadowed theirs. But even to the end they were the great ministers of Burma. Their acts speak for them.

CHAPTER III

THE DEATH OF KING MINDON

INTO his private and family affairs King Mindon did not introduce so many reforms as into the public affairs of his country. Perhaps it is easier to reform a government than to reform a family, to change a law than to change a custom. A law may be passed to-day and repealed to-morrow, but customs are of long growth, of slow change ; they alter, but they cannot be altered. And so King Mindon lived very much as his fathers had lived before him.

He had four chief wives who were queens, and many lesser wives. The lesser wives were chosen where the king wished. If the king saw a beautiful girl and desired her she became his wife ; if a tributary prince offered his daughter to the king she was accepted as a lesser wife. How many wives the king had I do not know. There were many, perhaps there were fifty of them ; there may have been more.

26

THE DEATH OF KING MINDON

Queens were far above the lesser wives and there were but four. It was the custom in Burma for the king to choose his chief queen, if not indeed all his four queens, from among his half sisters, the daughters of his father. This had been a custom in many nations, in Assyria, in Egypt, and among the Incas in Peru. Only a wife of equally royal blood could be a worthy consort to the king, could be a worthy mother of kings to come. And where could such be found but among half sisters to the king?

And so King Mindon took to himself, as his father had done before him, his half sisters to be queens, and many beautiful women to be lesser wives, daughters of Shan princes, of wealthy merchants, of officials. Many of these are dead now, many are alive yet, of all of them I need mention two only. These are the Laungshe princess, the mother of him who afterwards became King Thibaw, and the Sinpyumashin, the famous queen-mother who was the mother of her who was after the famous Queen Supayalat.

Of the Laungshe princess little seems to be known. She was of royal blood, a half sister to King Mindon and she had one son King Thibaw; she seems to have fallen into disgrace and to have lived and died in obscurity.

The Sinpyumashin, who was at King Mindon's death the chief queen, was also his half sister. She had no son, but she had three daughters, and all of them became queens to King Thibaw. There was Supayagyi or the great princess, Supayalat or the middle princess, and Supayagalè or the little princess. It seems to me that in her and her daughters centres all that is most wonderful, most striking in that seven years' drama that came to an end in 1885. It has been a tradition among the chief queens of Burma to be able to share equally with their husbands the weight of empire, to make their influence felt in the councils of the nation, and that the later queens of Burma were no degenerate daughters this history of my maid of honour will show.

The Sinpyumashin was a woman of great resource, of great courage, going straight to her end careless of all the world besides, as is the way of women. Her great ally was the Kinwun Mingyi, and they had much in common, for their views of life were the same.

With able ministers, with many wives, with many children, King Mindon lived and reigned in his new palace of Mandalay. He was the strong man who kept his house ; in his time there was no trouble. A rebellion that his son raised was quickly suppressed and the nation was at peace. All his reign of twenty-four years did Upper Burma enjoy happiness and prosperity, and at last full of years and honour, King Mindon was gathered to his fathers.

In European countries where we have feudal customs and the right of primogeniture there is no doubt as to who will succeed to king. The king dies, and his eldest son becomes king; he is accepted by all as the rightful claimant to the crown. But in these countries it is not so. To be the eldest son is no sure title to a kingdom, or indeed to anything, save to his share of the paternal property. All sons are much alike, and the eldest has no exclusive claims.

It is true that King Mindon had nominated an heir, a prince of the eastern palace, who was to be king when his father died; and had the prince lived it is probable there would have been little trouble. But he died.

Before King Mindon died the prince had gone, and when the king lay upon his death-bed there was no prince to whom was ensured the succession of the throne.

There were all sorts of stories afloat about the last illness of the king. He is said to have been poisoned at the end, and the names of those who

did it are given freely. There is not probably any
truth in these reports. Illness and death come
very suddenly in the East, and as the doctors are
not very wise, it is the custom to attribute an
unknown disease to poison or witchery.

There was no one who had any interest in the
king's death, but very many whose chance in life
lay entirely in his living. And so I do not think
that these reports are worth consideration. But
the king was ill, and very quickly he became ill
unto death. It is said that the king himself did
not care who should succeed him. Perhaps he was
too weary, too sick, to take much interest in those
things. The ministers would choose one of his
sons, the wisest and the most influential and the
best, to be king when he was gone. And this son
was to take for his chief queen the Salin princess.
She was the daughter of the king, and her he loved
above all his children, so that upon his death-bed
his only care was for her. Whoever would be
king she must be queen, that was all that the king
desired.

There is a curious story told of this princess
to explain how it was that she was beloved by the
king above all his children. It is said that in her
was incarnated the spirit of the king's mother. As
a little child she talked and acted as if this was so.

She knew things that only the king's mother could know, she remembered events that only the king's mother could have remembered. And when she was about four years old she was taken into the apartments of the dead queen to test her truth. Now these apartments had been kept carefully locked up ever since the queen-mother's death. No one had been allowed to enter them, they were left just as they had been when inhabited. And when the child was taken in she looked around and remembered everything. "There," she said, " is where I sat, there is where I slept. On that shelf you will find my silk dresses that I liked most, in that box are my jewels. They are of this pattern and of that." Thus spoke the child. And as she said so they found it. There was no doubt that it was the queen-mother's voice that spoke.

So the child was honoured above all the other children. She was called "queen" while the others were but princesses and she was destined to be the wife of the future king. She was plain, it is said, with small eyes, quiet and demure, not a girl that men cared for, but her father loved her above all his children.

About the bed of the dying king there was plot upon plot, and intrigue upon intrigue as to who should succeed him.

King Mindon had many sons and nearly all of these had little parties in the state, little cliques that wished to make their patron king. The most prominent of these were the Mekaya prince and the Nyaungok prince, men who were older than Prince Thibaw and who had great influence through their relations and their wives' relations in the palace. There were two great parties, one for each of these princes, and there was a third party amongst many of the ministers who did not desire a king at all just yet.

" The king's sons," they said, " are yet young, and no one is well known, no one is wise enough to receive from the strong hands of his father the sceptre of the kingdom.

" Therefore it will be better to wait. Let us have a regency. Here are all the king's ministers who have grown old in his service and know how a kingdom should be ruled. We shall manage the kingdom, and later on when the king's sons are men and have shown what manner of men they are, it will be easier to appoint one of them to be king. Burma is not as it used to be, cut off from the world and safe behind its mountains, but it is threatened by a great enemy who is very close. It is necessary for the government to walk very warily lest it fall."

Many of the wisest men in Burma were of this party.

But there was a fourth party yet. The Sinpyumashin was now head queen, the last of the four queens, and there was no one whose influence was so great as hers. Had she had a son no doubt he would have been king, no doubt she would have ruled the country through him, and been the power behind the throne greater than the throne itself. But she had no son, and therefore there was but one thing to be done, to choose a prince whom she could manage and to make her daughters his wives. And so it happened that her choice fell upon Prince Thibaw. There were many circumstances that pointed to him as a suitable prince. He was good-tempered it was known, easy going and unambitious, a man who would be easily led, who would quickly surrender power into any hands stretched out to grasp it. And he was learned. Of all the princes, he was the only one who had passed the great examination in classic literature, success in which brought so much honour for ever. A commoner who passed the examination was paraded through the city with music and acclamations. To have such a prince for king would conciliate many of the religious.

His mother too was of royal blood, whereas

most of the princes were sons of common mothers, and that was in itself a great recommendation in two ways.

It clearly ennobled Prince Thibaw, and it was the reason that he had no great following among the ministers and governors. With the Mekkaya and the Nyaungok princes it was different. They had a great crowd of relatives, and if either of them were made king it was most likely he would listen to the counsels of his relatives and the power would fall into their hands.

Therefore many things pointed to Prince Thibaw as the most fit for the succession, the most fit for the purposes of the queen-mother; and two days before the king's death he was so proclaimed.

What part the dying king had in the appointment of Prince Thibaw I do not know, and whether he even heard of it is uncertain. On October 28, 1878, at eventide, he died. His death was very sudden—so sudden that no one was prepared for it, no one had made the necessary preparations for what was to happen afterwards, to prevent the trouble that would certainly arise. As long as the king was thought to be alive there would be peace; at the news of his death all the varying discordant interests would awake and fight. If the queen mother and her party were to succeed in their plans they must act, and act quickly, ere the news was spread. And so, until their designs were matured, the news of the king's death was concealed, and rapid and secret action was taken.

Messengers were sent all about the palace in great haste to the king's children. "The king is very ill. He is dying, and before he dies he wishes to see you." So the message ran. All through the golden corridors the order went that the king's children should come swiftly to their father's side. Others were called too, officers and ministers. In the soft tropic night they came in twos and threes, awakened suddenly from their sleep. All the king's sons who were in the palace, and some of the daughters, came to see the last of the king their father. The great chamber outside the bedroom of the king was crowded with men, with women, with children, even with babies. Many were crying. King Mindon was a good father, he was much beloved of all his children.

It is I think difficult for us to realise all it meant to them, this death of King Mindon.

With us a king dies, a king succeeds ; it makes not very much difference, except sentimentally, even to his children. But here, to the loss of a father was added the loss, perhaps, of all that made life worth living, very likely of life itself. To that crowd, waiting there to see the dying moments of their father, all the world beyond was buried in ignorance.

A king, a convict, a corpse—who could tell what the day would make for each of them ?

They waited there in the great ante-chamber full of wandering shadows, lit with uncertain lamps that threw strange gleams across the carvings and the gold. They waited there, a sad crowd of men and women, but boys and girls almost all of them, waiting to be called to the bedside of their father, waiting the signal that was to call them to a last word with him. As they waited the corridors filled up with armed men, the doors around were closed, sentries with drawn swords were seen to stand at each entry of the great room. The silence of the ante-chamber of death was broken by the rattle of steel, the movement of armed men. While they gazed at it wondering what it all meant, in fear, in quickly growing dread, there came to them, not the messenger from their dying father, not one to call them to his side, but an officer with far different words. "The king is dead," he said; "King Mindon is dead an hour ago, and Thibaw is king now. We have heard that you are plotting against him, or may plot, and so you are all prisoners. Take them away."

He waved to the guards and the guards took them. Almost all the men and boys, children to King Mindon, that were in the palace were arrested on that fatal night. But two escaped. They were all led away to prison, and next day Prince Thibaw was brought from his monastery and made king.

So died King Mindon, wisest of all the kings, and Thibaw his son reigned in his place.

CHAPTER IV

THE NEW KING AND QUEEN

KING THIBAW was born in 1859 and so he was nearly twenty years of age when he came to the throne. His recent years had been passed in a monastery and from thence he was translated to a palace. All who know the life of Buddhist monks will appreciate the contrast. For laws of the monasteries are very strict and very stringent and cannot be broken by any one. To eat but one full meal a day, to abstain from all smoking and of course from all liquor, to wear only the yellow garment, to preserve always a sobriety of demeanour, never to look upon the face of a woman to admire her, these are some of the rules of the monkhood. And Prince Thibaw was a good novice and observed the laws and worked hard at his books, every one tells you that. He was a pleasant boy, good humoured and kind hearted, hating to be worried about things,

38

liking to take the world easily, very amenable
to influence.

Every one speaks well of him while he was a
boy. Then suddenly he came to the throne.
There was no interval. He came straight out of
the monastery and became a king, straight from
the self-denial and world-denial of a monk to unlimited power. For submission was exchanged
command, for absolute poverty great wealth, for
self-restraint the possibilities of complete self-
indulgence, all between the setting of one sun and
the setting of the next.

Can any worse training be imagined for a king
than this? He came to be king absolute in power,
and of all that it behoves a ruler to know he was
completely ignorant; of his country, his people, their
wants and desires, of foreign nations, their power
and ambition, he knew nothing whatever.

He was but a big school boy put upon a throne
and told to govern, a boy monk wholly dependant
upon those about him. And so King Mindon died
and Prince Thibaw was brought to the palace and
declared king. So far all the plans of the queen-
mother and the ministers had gone well. Thibaw
was king and the rival princes were safely locked
up, there was no immediate sign of trouble to
come.

King Thibaw would marry the queen-mother's daughter the great princess, and through her would the queen-mother govern the kingdom. The Salin princess was forgotten. Her father was dead and she had no one to help her, and promises are easily broken when there is no reason to keep them. After King Mindon died no word was ever said of the Salin princess.

The queen-mother had three daughters, the great princess, the middle princess and the little princess. The king was of course to marry the great princess as his chief wife. That was all settled. Of this girl Supayagyi but little is generally known. She seems to have been a quiet biddable girl, willing to do what she was told, ready no doubt to be wife to her half brother the king. She was about the same age as the king.

The second daughter Supayalat was a year younger than the king, a girl such as her mother had been before her, proud and passionate, loving and ambitious. All the nineteen years of her life she had loved Prince Thibaw. As children in the palace they had played together and loved each other, and as they grew older the love grew stronger. When Prince Thibaw went to live in the monastery the girl did not forget him. Though she might not see him yet she remembered him always. When-

ever she could she would send him a message, a
letter, a little present. There are not many things
a monk may receive, but all she could she did.
New robes and sweet food, and books, and above
all loving words, such did the middle princess send
to the young prince in the monastery. No one then
ever dreamt that he would be king.

Then of a sudden the boy monk became a king.
Within two days he was changed from an unknown
prince, one amongst very many, and became king.
He came to the palace and it was known at once
that he was to marry the great princess. She was
to be his queen, and in a short time they would be
married, all was arranged.

And the middle princess, the girl who had loved
him all her life, what was she to do? The king
could not marry her, for she was but a second
daughter. She must be thrust aside and be
forgotten too. What could a girl of nineteen do
against the customs of a nation, the rights of an
elder born, the arrangements of a government?
What does love weigh in the balance of a policy?
It is lighter than a feather, not worth regarding.
As the Salin princess had been put aside so would
the middle princess. Girls must suffer that
kingdoms may stand. It was hardly worth thinking about. I am sure that in all the palace, in all

the nation, no one thought twice of the middle princess and her disappointed love, no one dreamt anything could come of it, except the middle princess herself.

And she, what could this child do alone against all the government to get her lover to herself? Well this is what she did. When she heard that the prince was made king, and was come to the palace, and was shortly to be married to the elder princess she sat down at once and wrote him a letter. She sent it to him on the same day that he came to the palace. She lost no time. This is what she wrote.

"The king," she said, "is now king and I his sister the middle princess rejoice with him. He has become king no one knows how. And now it is said that he will take to be his wife the great princess my sister. And yet if the king stops to think this will not be so. Did my sister ever care for the king? What did she ever do for him? When the king was sent away from the palace to be a monk, did she write to him, did she send him money and presents? Where are these letters and these presents? Are they to be found anywhere? The king knows it is not so. There was no one who wrote to the king but me the middle princess. No one ever remembered him, no one ever sent him presents but me. Who can number the letters I have written to the king or measure the love that I bear to him ? These are beyond knowledge. Let then the king consider in his heart, let him call back the memories of the past and he will be sure that he can have no queen but me."

Something like this, says my maid of honour, was the message the girl princess sent to the boy king. "You see, Thakin, that she loved him very much. There are many people who say that she only wanted to be queen. I do not think this is true. She always loved Prince Thibaw when no one ever supposed he would be king. I am sure that if he had not been king at all she would have married him just the same. It was the man she wanted, not the king. Of course that he was king was so much the better.

"Thakin, I lived near the queen for four years. I saw her every day, and I am quite sure that this is true. In everything that happened till the end, there was always this first, that she loved her husband, that she wanted to keep him all to herself, not from desire of power, but from sheer affection and jealousy, and whatever she did in the kingdom, whatever advice she gave, whatever acts she committed, she thought first of the honour of her king.

"She was very self-willed, very ambitious, very

43

passionate, very cruel sometimes, but of all her passions this was greatest, her passion for the king.

"She could not bear that any one, even her elder sister, should take first place with the king. She wanted the first place, she wanted the second place also, she wanted all the places.

"She wrote to the king, and sent messages to him not to marry any one but her."

What the king replied I do not know, but a little later in the day the middle princess left her mother's rooms and went to the king. Straight to the king's apartments she went, and she stayed.

When the queen-mother heard the news she was furious. The conduct of her daughter the middle princess was unheard of, impossible. She went to the king and demanded that her daughter should be returned; she ordered the girl to come, never doubting of course that the boy monk that she had raised to the throne would do as she told him; that this daughter of hers would obey her mother as before. But she was mistaken. It was of no use. The girl would not go, nor would the king order her to do so. As she wished to stay, she should stay, so said the king. All the queen-mother's threats and expostulations were in vain.

When the ministers remonstrated with the king

they had no better success. They pointed out
that this was contrary to all law, to all custom,
to all tradition. The king must marry the elder
daughter, only she could be chief queen. And
then after that, after he had married the great
princess as custom ordered that he should do, he
could take the middle princess to be his second
wife. Meanwhile let the king send back the girl
to her mother. So said the ministers. The king
could not now on the very day of his accession so
outrage all decency in this way.

But it was of no use. While the ministers
talked the king looked in the girl's eyes, and when
they had finished he refused them roundly.

"If she wishes to go then shall she go," said the
king, "but if she will stay then shall she stay with
me for ever." In the face of this the ministers
were powerless.

The king was king and his will was law. If he
said no, then would no one do anything. That
was how the middle princess came to be queen in
place of her elder sister, in defiance of all the palace
people.

She came to the king, and the king took her and
never again were they separated. Such a thing
had never been heard of in all the kings' reigns
before until now, that an elder sister should be

dispossessed by a younger, and that the latter should make herself queen.

Yet this was but the beginning.

From that day the queen grew in strength and influence until in time there was no one in all Burma but only the queen.

What she wished the king ordered, and what the king ordered all people must obey. What was the source of her power no one can say.

She was not beautiful. Even my maid of honour admits that. "She was not beautiful, Thakin, but she was a queen. Women far more beautiful than she was faded before her into nothingness. And her eyes. Ah, Thakin, who- ever had eyes like the queen? Like pools of deep brown water, so large, so wonderful, but with a flame deep down in them that made one fear. She always cared for herself to make herself admired, her manners to those she loved were as the charm of a magician. And her voice was as clear as a silver gong thrilling across the evening waters where all is still. No one ever did but one of two things: they either loved her for ever or hated her as men hate and fear death. For she was very proud and very fierce, and when she hated she never forgave. There were two things that she could never abide: any attempt to wean the king from her, or any insult to his dignity. Whenever she heard that any woman was trying to come between her and the king she became like a mad thing; there was nothing she would not do. When any one tried to reduce the king's power or glory she would never allow it. Easier would death be than suffer such things."

That is what my maid of honour says of the queen. It must never be forgotten that she came to the throne as a girl of nineteen and was but twenty-six when the empire came to an end. Her power belonged of right to another, her husband's love belonged by custom to as many sweethearts as he liked to take. All her life in the palace she had to fight, to hold her power against enemies, to hold her lover from mistresses.

She did both to the end. Had she lived two thousand years ago in other conditions of things surely she would have gone down into history as one of the greatest of all queens. But she was born too late.

CHAPTER V

THE MASSACRES

It was in October 1878, as I have said, that King Thibaw and his queen came to their throne of Mandalay. Two days after King Mindon's death King Thibaw was proclaimed king and took the place of his father. The power, of course, remained in the hands of the queen-mother and the old ministers who had been with the old king. This novice fresh from a monastery, full of wise maxims, and of little else that belongs to wisdom, was not of the fibre to seize upon the reins of government, and make his rule felt. He was put upon the throne to be a puppet and under one guiding hand or another, he remained so all his life.

The queen's time was not yet come. Even for a woman of her strength of will, of her directness of purpose, it took time to deprive the old ministers of their power, to convince the queen-mother that in future she was to take a second place. And so

48

for some time, these children that had lit upon a throne by chance were but as royalties at play. They played about the steps of the throne, but did not govern.

The first news of the reign in Burma that reached the outer world, 'and astonished and horrified it, was the report that early in 1879 all the king's brothers had been executed. Not the king's brothers only, but their wives, and not grown people alone, but children. Men and women, boys and girls, even the infants at the breast, nearly all those who were arrested that fatal night in Mandalay, were executed.

I have heard from one who was at Mandalay at that time, that there had been for days rumours flying about. It was said that there was about to be a rebellion, that many people did not assent to Prince Thibaw being king, and that there would be a revolution. Many influential men it was stated had given in their adherence to one or another of the princes, and determined to release them. How much truth there was in all this I cannot say. There are those who say that all this was a mere pretence got up by the queen-mother and the palace clique to excuse their subsequent actions. There are those who emphatically affirm that all these plots were true. " There have always been plots," they say. " Did not the Mingoon prince rise against his brother King Mindon and occasion terrible trouble ? Have other princes, or more especially their adherents, ever agreed to the king-ship of one brother ? Is not all history full of such rebellion ? There were innumerable plots to put this prince or that on the throne, all agreeing that first of all King Thibaw must be deposed and the palace clique of queen-mother and ministers destroyed."

In prison with the captive princes were many leading men. There was a fully arranged design to break the prison, and then to attack the palace. Which story is true I cannot say.

Then came what are called the massacres. All the sons of King Mindon and their families and many other men too were executed. It happened at night. " On that night," says my informant, "there was a great hush over the city and town of Mandalay. A great fear of unknown horrors. Men kept to their houses in fear. In streets where at other times you would hear music and see dancing there was darkness and silence. No one knew what was happening. There under cover of the night horrible things were done. It was as if death brooded over the great city, and no one knew but what he would be taken ere dawn. No one slept all that night.   In the darkness of their houses they listened and watched."

All King Mindon's sons who could be found were executed.   Only two, the Nyaungok and Nyaungyan princes, escaped.   The British resident saved their lives and took them to Lower Burma. In after years these princes tried to get up a rebellion against King Thibaw and upset the government, but their attempts failed.   If there had been seventy sons left alive, there would have been no doubt pretty nearly seventy invasions and rebellions. It was to prevent this that the massacres occurred. For there is no doubt that for the peace and safety of the kingdom nothing could have been better than this execution of all claimants to the throne.   In such a kingdom a king has duties and responsibilities.   He is of some use.   A prince is of none. He is a mere expense to the people and a danger to the throne.   Any prince's life that fell then, meant that a hundred, perhaps a thousand, lives were saved to the nation, lives of merchants and soldiers, of ministers and peasants.   In King Thibaw's reign there was no serious rebellion, no wholesale destruction of villages, no confiscation of lands and proscription of rebels.   There was as far as that goes, peace, and it was bought with the blood of the sons of King Mindon.

It may be said that they would not themselves have raised rebellions, that many of them were quiet and peace-loving, only too glad to be allowed to live in obscurity. That may be true, and it may not. It makes but little difference. They would have been made the figurehead of plots despite themselves. Every one who had a grudge against the government would have declared he was acting in the name of one or other of the princes. Each brother of King Thibaw would have been, willy nilly, the focus of intrigue and trouble. And the people themselves understand this. I have heard it spoken of many and many a time in the villages when work was over and cigars were lit in the warm dusk. It saved the kingdom from much trouble, from ceaseless unrest and uncertainty. From the people's standpoint it was a good thing, although, of course, they could not approve of it. And from the standpoint of the royal family? Well, it is one of the prices a family pays for having unlimited power. It is the price that autocrats have had to pay for their power, this eminent necessity that all rivals must be put aside. History tells us but one tale about this. East or west has not differed, save that in the East the families are larger, the slaughter therefore heavier.

Where power and authority lie in the king and

not in the people, there can be but one end to possible rivals. And so when we consider the execution of the king's brothers we must not allow ourselves to be carried away by sentiment, but look the matter fairly in the face. There is now no object in raising a howl against the government of Burma. It is gone and dead. Let us therefore admit that this massacre was a necessity, a terrible one no doubt, but necessary.

Who was responsible for it I am not certain. What does it matter now to inquire? But of this I am assured, the young king and the girl who was become his queen were innocent. They knew nothing till all was over. And when he heard, the king sat down in his golden palace and wept. "My brothers," he said, "are dead because I am king. Surely I would never have been king had I known that this must happen."

So King Thibaw mourned for his brothers that were slain. He was a kind-hearted boy, and this was a most bitter, most terrible thing that had happened to him. While he was reposing in his new grandeur, giddy with the glory that had come to him suddenly and unexpectedly, he found that he must pay a bitter price for it. The steps of his throne were the corpses of his father's sons. Could there be a more terrible awakening from a young

dream of greatness and of love than this was ? He
never quite forgot it. But his throne was safe.
After this there was no doubt as to who was king.
Thibaw was lord of the golden palace, and of all
the white elephants, the king of kings. His
ministers were the Taingda and the Kinwun
Mingyis, and the power behind the throne, the
power that was to move the king as she willed, who
should it be but the queen-mother ? She it was
who had put the king on his throne, who had
secured the throne to him in safety, who was
mother of his wife. It seemed indeed as if the
queen-mother was to be supreme. And so the
king was king, and, for a time, the queen-mother
and the ministers ruled the kingdom.

But before very long there was a change. As
soon as the young queen felt herself firm upon the
throne, as soon as she had time to look about her,
she began to act. Then was it soon known that
there was to be no one in the kingdom but her.

She talked to the king. "Maung, Maung," she
said, "do you know all that is going on about you ?
Do you understand what is happening? You think
you are king, but is it so ? I think not, but that
the ministers are really the kings. They have
divided the kingdom. Each has taken to himself
part of what is yours. See now, how one minister

is in charge of the river and all boat business. All that concerns these subjects comes to him, and he passes orders. As far as these go he is king. And one minister is over the revenue, and another over the foreign affairs, and another over justice, and another over war. So is the kingdom divided up. You are king but in name. Let us stop all this."

As the queen said, so the king did. Gradually all power was withdrawn from the ministers and came into the king's hands, into the hands of her who was behind the king. The ministers' orders were disregarded, their authority destroyed. If a man was condemned by an order of a minister, he had but to appeal to the queen to be freed. "Let him go," she said. "Who is a minister to order such a thing?" She took a delight in thwarting and snubbing the ministers. There was to be no one in all the kingdom but her, and all were to know it. She was the very spirit of jealousy incarnate.

The ministers who were trained under the wise old king to know their work and to do it were rendered powerless, and the queen tried to govern by herself. She rejected even all advice. It was an impertinence. Nay, more, a minister had but to suggest anything to have it rejected at once;

and a girl who has never been out of a palace, who is as ignorant as can be, how can she rule a kingdom ? She could not do it.

Gradually the kingdom went back from the happiness of King Mindon's time, and trouble came upon it. For one thing, there were bad seasons. The rain failed, and the crops were short, and so the people suffered. Upper Burma was never a rich country ; now it became poorer. With short crops came restlessness. Farmers were ruined, and took to evil ways of living. Crime increased, and it was not suppressed. In King Mindon's time if crime increased in any district the governor was held responsible, and unless the trouble was quickly dealt with he came to grief. The local officials were afraid of the king, and knew he was well informed.

But under the boy king the local officials again raised their heads. They did not care very much for Mandalay, they were aware that the king was only so in name, and they became slack in the performance of their duties. Bands of robbers increased until whole districts were held in terror and paid blackmail to one brigand leader or another. The officials did nothing. Indeed it is said that many of them were in the pay of the brigands and protected them from harm in case they happened to be arrested. Justice became degraded and the law was forgotten.

The revenue in consequence suffered, and the soldiers and others could not be paid. Then they also had to prey upon the country and matters became worse. It is a sad story how the nation which had been prosperous and happy under King Mindon fell into misery and lawlessness so soon afterwards.

When a government is all centred in the king and everything depends upon him, then, should he not prove a strong man, all authority is gone. And the king was a boy. It is doubtful how much he knew of what was going on, whether he could have done anything, even had he known and understood. The country became a prey to the palace clique. Places were openly sold to the highest bidder and then he was disgraced in order that the place might be again sold. It was somewhat of the principle of the Borgia and his Cardinals. Justice became a scoff and was a matter of money.

The border tribes broke out. Feeling that the strong hand that held them so firmly was gone, they raided into Burma. On the north the Kachins, and on the west the wild Chins threw off their subjection and attacked the country of their sovereign. They were only repulsed with loss and great difficulty and the yoke that they had thrown off could not be re-enforced. The allegiance of the Shan princess in the east became doubtful.

Everywhere was evident that the strong hand and wise brain that had ruled the country so well was laid to rest. Of course all this did not happen at once. It takes time both for a country to improve and to deteriorate. I am looking far ahead, almost to the end of the kingdom, when I say that the country became a prey to brigand bands. But the change began to be felt very soon after the king's death, and the evil grew year by year. No doubt in time the nation would have refused to submit to such a state of things any longer, and there would have been a change of some sort. It is impossible now to guess what that change would have been. For no time was given. Another nation stepped in and subdued the kingdom.

CHAPTER VI

DAYS IN THE PALACE

IT was not till nearly two years after the king's accession that my maid of honour came into the palace ; a child of nine years old, maid to a queen of twenty-one. And this was the way of it. She was not an Upper Burman at all. She was born away south in British Burma, in Tavoy, and there she lived through her early childhood. When she was nine years old her father, who was a China-man, came to Upper Burma to live and began to take up contracts for the government. He built amongst other things the round tower with the winding stair at the south-east corner of the palace. He would have been a rich man she says if he had received all the money due to him. But he was never paid and now he is dead and the money is lost. He knew many people in the palace, and so after a time his little daughter was accepted as maid of honour to the queen.

59

"There were other maids of honour," she says. "The king had maids of honour, and the queen-mother had maids of honour also. But they were not nice, not the same as we were who were the queen's own maids."

She is very proud, I think, of having been maid of honour to the queen, and when she speaks of it she flushes with a little flush of pride, for it seems to her to have been a great thing. "None of the other maids of honour were the same as we were. The maids of the queen-mother were such as we did not care to know. Many of them were very curious, wild Shan girls and Chin girls, all sorts of girls, some with tattooed faces. So ugly, Thakin, they were, and they had no manners at all. The queen's mother and her maids lived on the north of the great throne room, and it was always untidy there. We did not see much of them.

"Then there were the king's maids of honour who had charge of his clothes. There were but few of them compared to us, and they were not so much esteemed as we were, for we were of the best.

"There were, I think, five or six hundred girls maids of honour to Mebya. They were divided into companies of thirty or forty, with one as head. My head was the daughter of the Taingda Mingyi, the old minister who brought on the war. Each company went on duty for six hours at a time, and the queen herself distributed the hours of service for each company.

" We lived by two and two in a room. All the little houses on the south of the western throne-room were our houses. Out of the windows you can see into the south garden, and there are steps near there to go down by. My first companion was Ma Mya, who was daughter to a governor somewhere in the north country. She took a husband afterwards and got into trouble and was sent away. The next companion of mine was Ma Shwe Tha.

"There was one European maid of honour, a Roman Catholic sister, and some of us were daughters of Shan chiefs and other princes. I think many were kept in the palace so that their fathers might keep true to the king. One of them came into trouble too. Shall I tell the Thakin how that was ? "

" Let that be afterwards," I said. " There is so much to tell. But tell me first of your life in the palace. You were only such a little girl when you went in. Did your mother not go with you to look after you ? "

She shook her head. "No. Of course she came sometimes, but I was quite happy. Ah !

Thakin, it was pleasant in the palace. There was my room-mate to help me, and there was our chief, the Mingyi's daughter, and there was the queen. She looked after us very carefully to see that nothing went wrong with any one, and would always listen to any complaint. She was very good to us. She gave each of us nine silk skirts a month to wear, and money besides to buy jackets and other things."

I suggested that this seemed a large number to wear out in a month, nine silk skirts in twenty-nine days, but she shook her head. Skirts got spoiled many ways, playing hide-and-seek in the palace gardens, and feeding the fishes—you were never allowed to wear an old skirt, even to go boating in ; it was always necessary to be smart before the queen.

The silks were usually pink and silver, but they varied. Of course on state occasions the queen wore the proper state dress, and so did the maids. This is a very elaborate, very beautiful dress, with a sort of helmet on the head. It is quite inde-scribable to those who have never seen it. The helmet has a curious effect in giving a soft childish expression to the face which is delightful.

But in ordinary life they wore much the same dress as Burmese women always wear. This is a short skirt of silk, usually in longitudinal stripes. At the top there is a piece of cotton of a different colour, usually purple. At the bottom is a piece of silk, of a very light greyish-pink, getting darker as it approaches the ground, where it ends in numerous little stripes. Whatever the main part of the dress may be, the top and bottom are generally the same. The skirt is open at the side and the leg shows a little, in walking, very prettily. The jacket worn in the palace was always white cambric, open in front, the jacket and skirt being so arranged as to give the appearance of a dress cut square at the bosom. There was always a bright kerchief to drape over the shoulder or carry in the hand, as the wearer thought most becoming. It is a very pretty dress, very graceful, very gay, matching so well their fair brown complexion, their merry laugh, their pretty coquettish manners. They wear almost always a pearl necklace about the throat and many gold bracelets. The hair is worn in a coil on the head with flowers in front, and of course their feet are bare. No shoes could be worn in the palace ; it was sacred ground. As we take off our hats, so do Orientals take off their boots when entering another man's house ; in so far, to-day here, is as it was two thousand years ago. Did not Abraham do the same ? Is it not done in every eastern country, even in Japan to-day?

So all the maids went barefooted in the palace, passing softly to and fro, their little feet making no sound on the solid pavement. The queen wore much the same dress as her maids, but there was this rule, that if she was wearing a dress of a certain design no princess nor maid might wear one of the same design on the same day.

"But how did you manage?" I asked. "Did you know beforehand what the queen would wear?"

"When we went on duty we would peep and see, hiding behind some one else. And if we found we had on a skirt like the queen wore, we would run away and change quickly and return.

"Ah, Thakin! it was very pleasant in the palace. There was but little work to do attending the queen, it was a pleasure not work. The maids read aloud to her sometimes, sacred books and books of plays, and every one would listen, and stories would be told. After a little time I was made to roll cigarettes for the queen. She smoked many cigarettes, just like the Thakin does. She did not like the Burmese cheroots. And so I would sit behind her and roll her cigarettes, and listen to her talk.

"The king was nearly always with her, sometimes

he went away to talk with the ministers or do
business or amuse himself with his pages, but
generally the king and queen were together. She
loved him so much, Thakin, the king her husband,
no one can say how much she loved him, and she
wanted always to be with him.

"Ah! Thakin, it was very pleasant in the
palace. There was always something to play at,
always so many to play with, all girls. No, of
course we were not allowed to have the pages to
play with. They kept to their place in the palace,
to their apartments and their duties, and we kept
to ours. I was young then and did not care, ah!
Thakin laughs and says it is not so now. Why
should the Thakin laugh; what if I have a sweetheart now? Is there any harm in that? Has
the Thakin never had a sweetheart? The Thakin
shakes his head, but ah! it cannot be true. We
played all our games among ourselves with the
queen and sometimes the king. We used to play
many games. There was hide-and-seek in the
gardens. One of us would hide, and the others
would come and look all over the place. Sometimes the girl who hid could not be found at all,
she would hide so well. The queen too would
hide and we would look for her. It was not a
proper thing to find the queen, and so the princesses

and the maids of honour would go wandering about and looking in all the wrong places."

"What happened if any one was rash enough to find the queen?" I asked. The girl laughed. It appears that when she first went to the palace and played hide-and-seek she found the queen. "For indeed it was easy enough. I could see her kneeling down on a little hill behind a clump of bamboos. Every one who looked could see. I went up and found her. I thought I was very clever."

"And then?"

"She boxed my ears. She was angry."

"I suppose you never found her again?" I asked.

"No. No one could ever find her but the king, if he were playing with us. Then after a time when she was tired of seeing us wander up and down and look in all the wrong places, she would come out laughing, and say she was too clever for us and some one else must hide. So one of us would hide and there would be great fun looking for her all up and down the gardens, in the boats, behind the rocks, or perhaps we would find her perched in a tamarind tree.

"Then we would go out in the boats. The fish were so tame that if you put some rice on the edge and tapped the bank and cried 'Hey, hey,' the fish would come crowding up and eat it. There

THE QUEEN PLAYING HIDE AND SEEK

were so many they would quarrel and fight and push each other about to get at the rice. Some had gold leaf on their heads. Once when the queen was in a boat with the king, a big fish jumped right into the boat, and the queen was delighted and laughed and screamed and took it up in her hands and put it back into the water. Her dress was all splashed over with water and mud but she did not mind that. We also used to catch crows."

"What did you do that for?" I asked.

"For fun. We would wait till a crow came into the room and rush and slam the doors. Then there would be great running about and climbing on tables and throwing handkerchiefs to fetch the crow down. He would fly to and fro for a long time, but at last he would get tired and we would catch him."

"What did you do then? Kill it?" I asked.

"Kill it?" she answered with great surprise, "what should we want to take its little life for? No, we would stroke it and give it some water to drink, and the queen would put gold leaf on its beak, or a ring on its foot or tie a string with something on it round the crow's neck, and let it go again. There was always a tremendous excitement among the other crows when this crow came forth. They would crowd round it and caw very

67

loudly, and the caught crow was ashamed. We never caught the same crow twice.

"If it was very hot and we could not go out, the queen would wrap a lot of things in paper—rings and gold and stones and feathers—and put them in a bag. The princesses and maids of honour drew the things out. When you got a ring or a jewel you were pleased and every one congratulated you. When you got a feather every one laughed. Oh, how ashamed you were!"

"Did you ever get a feather?" I asked.

"No. I never got a feather, but I got a piece of tobacco-leaf once. Every one laughed, and the queen said: 'That is very proper; she makes my cigarettes, of course she should get tobacco.' On another occasion I got a small gold ring. I have it now, Thakin. It is not worth much."

It was a little ring of plain gold with a small ruby in it roughly set. It was not worth much, as she said.

"The stone," she continued, looking down at it sadly, "is not very bright. But you can see down into it, and it is full of lights, full of memories of long ago. I shall never forget the day when I got it. We were all there: the king and the queen and all the maids of honour. Ah, how we laughed, and how we enjoyed ourselves! This ring is full of pleasant memories. I have another jewel the queen gave me full of memories that are very sad, but this is full of pleasure.

"Those are the sort of games we used to play every day, but at certain times we had great festivals. Three times a year there was a great amusement, throwing water at each other. A low bamboo barrier was put up in the garden, and the queen and her maids were on one side and the king and his pages on the other. We got water in little cups out of the moat and threw it, one side at the other. We got very wet, and we were not allowed to wear old dresses, but quite new ones. They were all spoilt of course."

"Who threw at the queen?"

"The king, and the queen threw water at him and we all threw water at the pages and ministers."

"And did the ministers and pages never cross over the barrier?"

"If any minister or page had crossed the barrier he would have been executed right off. No one did, of course. No. Girls never crossed to the men's side. How can you ask such questions, Thakin? The barrier was put up to prevent it.

"Then twice a year money would be thrown by the king for the people to scramble for. He would throw fifty thousand rupees or more. One man

got thirty rupees or fifty rupees. It was such fun
to see them scrambling. All the soldiers would
come and the attendants, men and women, and
make a great crowd and fall over each other in
their haste to get the money. Where a handful of
rupees fell twenty people would fall one on top of
the other, scrambling and struggling and laughing.
Oh, Thakin, it was such fun, you have no idea."

She clapped her hands. " We all used to laugh :
the king and queen and everybody laughed till they
could not laugh any more."

" What did you get ? "

" I was a maid of honour, one of the queen's
maids of honour," she replied somewhat severely,
drawing herself up. "The Thakin does not
suppose that the maids of honour scramble for
money ? "

That was how they spent their days in the
palace, this king who was twenty-two years old
and this queen of twenty-one. They played as
children play who do not care, who are happy in
the day and do not think of to-morrow. Surely it
most have been pleasant in the palace.

CHAPTER VII

EVENINGS IN THE PALACE

I ASKED, "What did you do in the evenings after the sun set and the ghosts came out in the gardens so that you could not stay there?"

"In the evenings," she answered, "we had pwès, marionette shows, and dramatic performances. We had them very often. The king would say: 'There is nothing to do; let us have a pwè.' And the queen would clap her hands and agree. So the dancers would be sent for, and they would dance all night in the great portico. The Thakin knows the place in the south of the palace. There is a great room there whose walls are glass panels enclosing flowers. We would sit up there in front of the room, the queen and the king and the princesses and ourselves. And down below would be the performers and a great ring about of the lower people of the palace, the guards and attendants. I have seen many plays there. If we only

71

had a little performance of perhaps only one dancer, then it was not held in the great portico, but in one of the rooms on the west of the palace. The Thakin has seen the king's dancer. She was very beautiful. She danced like a grass stem swaying in the wind. We often had her to dance in the palace. There were so many dances and performances in the palace, I forget them all, only the last great one at the end, two days before the fall. That I remember always, but the others I forget.

"When we did not have a pwè we would sit and talk. The maids of honour would tell stories. Those who came from far parts would tell very strange stories of things in their country. They said there were devils sometimes in the hills, and all kinds of snakes and tigers. Thakin, did you ever see a tiger?"

"Oh yes," I answered, "once or twice at a distance."

"And a devil?"

"No," I said; "never a devil; are there devils?"

My maid of honour opened her eyes wide. "Of course. There are several kinds of devils. I never saw one at all, but I saw the spirit of a tree once."

" You did ? " I asked. " What was he like ? "

" He was all white and shining, and he stood under the great tree and looked at me. I was not afraid at all. I told the queen about this one evening, when we were all telling stories, and she said she would like to see one too.

" The girls from the Shan country told very strange stories and the European maid of honour also told stories. She said that in her country all the rivers turned into ice in the winter, so it must be very cold. I do not know how the people live. And she said there were no teak trees in that country, so the houses must be very poor. I felt quite sorry for the people there, Thakin. She said that in the winter it was only light for about seven hours in the day, and sometimes for two months you would not see the sun. Is that true ? "

" Oh yes," I said, " it's true enough."

" She must have been very glad to live in Burma, I should think, where we have always sunlight and it is warm, Thakin. Many other stories too, she told me, but some we could not believe because they were too hard. I liked the stories our own people tell best. I remember, Thakin, one very curious story a maid of honour told us one evening in the palace. She was a girl from away in the north where they seem to have more curious things than here. She said there was a man there, who was a toddy climber, climbing up the great palms to get the juice. He was the son of a man who owned many palms, and so was well off.

"One day he had an accident. When he was climbing up a tree the frail bamboo ladder broke, and he fell down flat on the ground. Some men who were in the grove some way off saw him fall, and supposed he was killed because he came down from so far up with such a crash. 'Ah, ah!' they said, 'there is Po San, falling off a tree, probably he will be killed; we must go and carry his dead body to his father.'

"They came running to the tree to pick up the body, but when they came there Po San sat up and looked at them. They were so surprised that their mouths remained wide open. Then Po San got up and said, 'What is the matter?' And the men said, 'Oh nothing, nothing at all, only we supposed you were killed, and we were about to carry your body to your father.'

"Then Po San said he wasn't in any way dead, and he didn't know what they came bothering about. He seemed quite annoyed, so the men went away again.

" Po San was to be married to a girl in the village, and as he did not seem at all hurt by his fall he was married all right.

" But soon his wife began to complain. He was not as he used to be. He used to be kind and good-natured, and very merry, but now he was stupid, and cross, and evil-tempered. Also he used to steal away at nights. When his wife would wake up at nights and stretch out her arm to feel for her husband that his presence might give her courage in the dark, she could not find him. So she began to get suspicious and think he must go after some girl instead of her. One night she made up her mind to watch him. She did not go to sleep, but only pretended, lying with her eyes shut and making her breath come very slow, and when Po San got up and went out, she crept after him. She expected that he would go to some house in the village, but he did not. He went through the village and crept through a hole in the fence and his wife followed him. The thorns scratched her, but she did not care. He went on through the field and at last he came to the grave-yard. His wife remained under a tree watching and she saw her husband go to a new grave and scratch up the ground, and pull up the body of a man recently buried. When he got the corpse

out he ate some of the flesh, and then put the body
back, and put the earth over it again. And his
wife understood what had happened.

"This was not her husband at all. When he had
fallen from the tree he had been killed, and because
when he was killed there was no one there to shut
his mouth, an evil spirit had entered into it. This
man she married was not Po San at all, but an
evil spirit, a pok; wasn't that a dreadful thing,
Thakin?"

"What did they do with him?" I asked.

"The woman reported it to the governor next
day, and the pok was killed.

"The queen when she heard the story said she did
not like it at all. She liked pleasant stories about
good spirits. Stories like this made us all afraid.
We were afraid to go about alone at night for fear
of poks and devils, and when we woke up in the
night we shivered. So when any one was about to
tell a story afterwards the queen would ask first if
it was a pleasant one before she allowed it to be
told.

"Those evenings were so pleasant, Thakin, in
the palace. When the queen was in a good temper,
and she generally was, she would laugh and talk
just like a girl. And the king would laugh and
talk too. The rooms were so beautiful with their

gold and their mirrors, and the lights that fluttered here and there as the wind came sighing through the great doors, and the maids were so pretty too, with their bright dresses and jewels, and it seems to me, looking back, like a fairy story. Ah, I was so happy in the palace. But one night I got a great fright, and this was the way of it.

"It was a night in the hot weather, it had been very hot all day, and even now at night it was hot, though the fans waved to and fro.

"The king was not there, and the queen and maids were not talking, but reading aloud from a sacred book, and it was very difficult to understand. I tried and tried, but it was full of hard words, and so I gave up trying, and began to watch the fans move to and fro, and try and count the diamonds on the queen's hands. I do not know how it was, but I fell asleep. I do not know how long I was asleep, but at last some one woke me. She pushed me on the arm and said, 'Wake up, wake up; the queen is speaking to you.' So I woke up all stupid and saw every one looking at me, and I felt dreadfully frightened. I didn't know what the queen would do to me for falling asleep. But she only laughed and held up her finger and said, 'You have been asleep.' When I tried to say something and could not find words, she went on, 'You are only a child to sit up so late. Go away to bed, you very sleepy little maid of honour.'"

My maid of honour laughed. She always laughs when she thinks and talks of those days, the cheerful laugh of a child.

"So I went away all by myself. I had never walked about in the palace alone before, and when I got away from the lights and sounds of the queen's room, I felt afraid. The palace was so still, and so high, and it was almost dark everywhere. So I walked at first very fast, and then I began to run, and so coming round a corner I ran into a door that was shut, and knocked all the breath out of me. There was a corridor there with big doors at both ends, more like a room than a corridor. The doors were always open before, and we went that way to our rooms, but on this occasion the doors were shut. I pushed against them and beat with my hands, for I was afraid that the dark was full of poks. 'Open,' I cried; 'open, please open.'

"I heard a moving inside and I hammered more. 'Open quick,' I cried; 'why are the doors shut like this?'

"At last the door opened just a little, and a man

looked out. I could not see who it was, because the light was behind him, and I could not see his face, but I was not afraid of men.

" 'Let me in,' I ordered. 'I want to pass through.'

"The man opened the door and came out. Then he shut the door behind him, and caught me by the ear.

" 'Who are you?' he said; " a little girl in such a hurry?'

" 'I am one of the queen's maids of honour,' I said, 'who am going to bed. Who are you shutting the doors?' I felt angry at this man stopping me when I was in a hurry, and I spoke crossly.

" 'Oh,' he answered, 'I am the king.'

" I was very much frightened to find it was the king, and I wanted to go down on my knees, but he held me by the ear. 'I didn't know,' I stammered.

" 'What did you come this way for?' said the king. 'Tell me truly. Did the queen send you?'

"Then I told the king it was because I was asleep, and the queen told me to go to bed, so I came this way. 'It is the short way to my room,' I said; 'may I go?'

" But the king said I must go round, that I could not go that way to-night. So I turned away and ran down the passage to go away round. The king watched me till I turned the corner. I looked back and still saw him standing there. Thakin, I did not think of it at the time. I was only a little girl. How could I guess what was happening? Even when two days later there was a great trouble, I could not guess."

" What was the trouble ? " I asked.

" It was about a Shan princess. I do not know all that happened, only the queen was very angry. The Shan princess was one of her maids of honour too, like me, only much older. And the queen was very angry. First she intended to have her killed, but then she changed her mind. I think the king must have spoken to the queen, for they spent a very long time together that day talking alone in the little white room by the fountain. But the Shan ` princess was taken into the gardens and beaten once or twice to dishonour her, and then thrust through the gates out of the palace.

" I do not know what became of her, but she never came back again. No one ever spoke of her any more. And for days after the queen was angry with the king, and the king was very much ashamed of himself. I think, Thakin, this was the first quarrel they had ever had. I was so sorry for the queen because her eyes were big with tears for several days, and though she was very cross to us, yet we were all sorry for her."

CHAPTER VIII

THE ENTHRONEMENT OF THE KING

"AFTER that no Shan princesses were allowed to come into the palace and be maids of honour to the queen. It was the custom always for the Shan princes to send their daughters to be wives to the king of Burma, but in future this was not to be. If any Shan princess came she was never allowed to be in the palace. She was either returned to the prince her father, or shut up in a sort of prison where no one was allowed to come. When the Shan princes heard how their daughters, whom they sent to be queens, were treated they became very angry. But the queen did not care. As long as the king was faithful to her she did not care who was angry. She was ready to do anything to keep him."

"It was hard on the princesses," I said.

And my maid of honour replied with a sigh, "Yes, it was hard on them. But the queen was afraid of herself; who could blame her? Any woman would do so, just as the queen did."

There was never any peace for the queen. She could never rest and shut her eyes and be sure that all would go well. She must watch always, lest the king her husband be taken from her, and she became but one wife among many. If sometimes the queen was called, with reason, cruel and revengeful, a woman who could not forgive, let this be remembered on her side, that she was fighting always for that which was more to her than life. There was always some danger pressing her, some imminent danger, that it took all her strength and all her will to avert. No sooner was the Shan princess disposed of than there arose a new peril.

It was necessary for the king to be enthroned, to go through that ceremony which to them was equivalent to our coronations. It was time that the king was king, there was no one else to dispute his power, his brothers were dead or in banishment, and he had no rival near his throne. But that was not sufficient. He must be crowned, there must be a great ceremony in the palace, and all the people must be called, and King Thibaw must there before his ministers and soldiers take the oaths that all the kings of Burma had to swear to. Until this was really done he was not king; he was but a *locum tenens* sitting upon a vacant throne, and his reign was not assured. To signify to the nations and to foreign powers that King Thibaw was in very truth in undisputed possession of the kingdom the ceremony must be performed.

But to do this the king must be married. Here was the trouble. The king must be married, so that when the oaths were taken he should have by his side a queen to share with him the responsibility of his promises, the glory of his power. And the middle princess could not be that queen; for she was but a second daughter. While the elder princess lived, the king could never publicly marry the middle princess. He might love her and take her as his wife, and give her all the power and all the glory of the queenship, but chief queen she could never be. Even the power of the king failed here. There was limit beyond which even the strength and courage of the middle princess could not carry her.

She had to bow her head to necessity, knowing perhaps that it was but a form, and though her sister might be carried into the palace as chief queen, yet that it would be but a shadow of grandeur, and that all the reality of power, of love, of possession would remain hers.

She consented to the wedding.

And so after two years of the king's accession to the throne, in the full moon of October 1880, King Thibaw was married to the elder princess.

The full moon of October is always a great feast in Burma. It is the end of the Buddhist Lent. The two months of fasting are over, and the rains' are gone, and the south wind is dead. The north wind is beginning to blow down life-giving coolness from the far-away hills, and the sky is become clear as a sapphire. With the full moon the fast ends and all the people rejoice.

On that day was King Thibaw married to the elder princess. It was a great ceremony, gay and beautiful and joyous as these people knew how to make their festivals, and all the palace was crowded with people.

It began as all festivals begin with presents to the monks. For no Buddhist can be happy until he knows that he has given of his wealth and of his property for the happiness of those who live about him, and purified his heart with charity, so that all may be well with him. Great offerings were made to the monks, of robes and of books, strange books written in golden letters on lacquered leaves and bound with crimson. Fruit there was too, and flowers, great heaps of flowers and food of all kinds. There are so few things a monk may receive that the choice of gifts is limited. And when the monks were satisfied there was yet left plenty for the people, for generosity is a virtue that people believe in here.

Then was formed a great procession, and the king and the elder princess were carried on their golden chair amid all the people, followed by the princesses and the maids of honour and the ministers wearing all their court costumes, a great crowd. The procession went through the gardens and up the steps of the palace to the great throne-room, guarded by many troops. There the king and the queen—she was now for a moment queen —were placed upon the throne, and the great multitude knelt before them and there was a dead silence.

Then the ministers read out the oaths. One by one they were read out, so that all the people could hear, and one by one the king and the queen swore to them.

They were such oaths as these : To be honour-able and just, to be kind hearted and free from revenge, to be peace loving and averse from blood-shed. The king swore to maintain the faith of the Buddha and remember the holy men, to keep the offices and courts of his nation free from all blame, to remember always that the people were his care,

and that the poor were to be cherished and not
ground down. All the oaths that the ministers
offered did the king accept. The people were
surprised at this; for his father Mindon, the great
king, had refused to swear some of the oaths.
"How can I refrain from bloodshed," cried King
Mindon, "and be a good king? The wicked must
be punished, and who can punish them but I the
king?" So King Mindon would not take all the
oaths.

But King Thibaw accepted them all and swore to
them before the people. And those that knew him
say that he meant them all—that as far as lay in
his power he kept them always to the end. No
one doubts but that he was an honest king.

After the ceremony there were feasts and dances
and amusements all the day, and all the night too.
Every one rejoiced that the king was at length
upon his throne, that he had taken to himself the
queen whom he would have. In all the palace there
was rejoicing and music and lights, and the laugh of
the people who are glad.

But the middle princess sat alone. All day she
sat alone in her room in the palace, waiting till the
king returned. Though the queen-mother and all
the princesses and all the maids of honour were at
the ceremony, yet would the middle princess not

go. "Ah, Thakin," says my maid of honour, "how could she go? For the king was hers, her very own. How could she go and see him sitting on the throne with another, or join in the train that followed another queen than herself? Some women might have done so, but the middle princess could not.

"All day she sat in her rooms in the palace with the shutters down, to shut out the sight of the many people passing and the sound of the music and the laughter. All were gone to the procession but she, and her rooms were empty. We were all ordered to the procession. But now and again some of us would come very quietly and enter the ante-chamber and peep into the room, afar off, in case that we were wanted. But she never noticed us. All day she sat quite still with eyes of stone, and even when they brought her food she did not notice. The night fell, and the moon came out, and there were great white beams across the darkness of the room, while outside all was as light as day. Half the night passed and the king did not come, because he was at the pwè in the portico. And then at last the king came. Though he was newly married that day to the elder princess, yet when the festivities were over he came straight back to the middle princess, without a thought of her who was become his chief queen."

THE ENTHRONEMENT OF THE KING

The elder princess was given the great state apartments that were for the reigning queen, and there she lived for a time. The queen's apartments were hers, and the name of chief queen, and that was all.

As for the middle princess, she did not want any rooms. Her rooms were the king's rooms, and with him she always lived. That the king had married the elder princess made no difference. It was because only of custom. And before long the elder princess lost even what she had. "Let her return," said the middle princess to the king. "What do we two want with her so near us?" And the king agreed. So the elder princess returned to the rooms of her mother, and the king never saw her again. Even her name abandoned her. She was queen but for a day, and after that there was no queen but the middle princess. If one spoke of the queen, that was whom he meant— the middle princess. There was no other queen but she.

CHAPTER IX

THE "STEAMER DOG"

"How was the palace furnished?" I asked. "Did the king go in for European furniture at all, chairs and tables and such things?"

"No," said my maid of honour, "the king and queen did not like to sit on chairs, nor did they care for furniture except just their own things. They sat on cushions covered with velvet and with silk. The only time they sat on a chair was when they played the big musical box that they had got from France. It was a very big box and it played our own Burmese tunes, such as they play at pwès. The queen was very fond of it, and the king too often played it in the evenings. It was very pretty, and went 'tink, tink, tink,' like a lot of silver bells on a pagoda.

"There were mats and carpets on the floors, some of which came from France, and there were great mirrors.

"These mirrors were very large, taller than a man, and you could see all of yourself at once in them. And they were so clear, it was like looking through very clear water at another person the same as yourself. The queen was very fond of looking at herself in these mirrors, and we too, yes, all of us liked to look at ourselves in the mirrors when we got a chance. But there was nearly being a sad catastrophe about these mirrors.

"The queen had a little dog, a very small beast with long silky hair and big ears and eyes. The queen was very fond of it, had taught it to sit up when she clapped her hands, and it was very clever. She always had it with her. One day it was lost.

"Such a search there was about that dog. People were going to and fro about the palace asking, 'Have you seen Mebya's little steamer dog?' (the queen was called Mebya) and every one was answering, 'No, I have not seen it.' I was asked about twenty times and I too went about and inquired. But no news could be obtained. The queen was in great distress. 'Who can have stolen my dog?' And every one assured her that no one could have possibly stolen her dog. 'Who could steal the queen's dog?' we answered; 'no one would steal it. The little dog must have fallen into the water and been eaten by a big fish, or it may have been carried off by a kite. Of course no one would take it.'

"It happened that next day the queen gave orders to move one of the mirrors. It had not been properly placed, and it must be taken away and put elsewhere. And when the mirror was moved the men found behind it, squeezed against the wall, the queen's little dog.

"One of the soldiers who had been moving the mirror came to the garden where the queen was with the dead little dog in his arms and told the queen about it. The queen was very sorry to see her dog dead and she took it in her hands and stroked it. And then she became very angry and said it was disgraceful carelessness on the part of the soldiers who had first put up the mirror. She would have them all executed at once, she said, because of their killing the dog by carelessness.

"'The king was very much disturbed when he heard the queen say this. He patted her soothingly on the shoulder and he said, 'Think now, Su, Su, what this is you are about to do. Here is only a little dog, and because it is dead, you would take the lives of perhaps twenty men. For these mirrors are very heavy, and many men must have been working at them.'

" 'Maung, Maung,' said the queen to the king, 'I do not think your soldiers are any better than animals, or they would not have let my little dog die like this. They ought to be executed.'

"But the king patted her shoulder again.

" 'You are angry now, Su, Su, but you would be dreadfully sorry to-morrow if you had a lot of men killed because of your dog. See now it was only an accident.'

"But the queen was very angry and moved away towards the palace to give the order to have the men executed, and the king went with her, speaking soothing words to her as she went. We all looked at each other in fear and followed behind, horrified at what the queen proposed to do. We all hoped that the king would succeed in quieting the queen. And he did. After he had talked to her for a little, she became more calm and she said that because the king asked her she would extend her mercy to the soldiers who had killed her little dog, but that they must be very careful in future. Then the little dog was buried in the garden, and soon we forgot all about him and the narrow escape the men had, who put the mirrors in the palace. But it gave us a great fright at the time.

"We often got frights in the palace. Things were always happening that made us afraid for some one or another, but when the danger was passed we quickly forgot all about it."

They breakfasted about nine o'clock, so my maid of honour told me, and they dined at four o'clock or five in the evening. At mid-day the queen would have a little luncheon of cake, Japanese cakes. She had a Japanese cook-woman who knew how to make sugar cakes which my maid of honour tells me were very good.

"The queen would give us some," she said, "when she was pleased with any of us. She was always ready to give things. She was very generous."

Their breakfast and dinner were just rice like those of other Burmans. "I never supposed," said my maid of honour, "that people could live on anything but rice. The king and queen ate rice, and, of course, there was curry too. It was brought in golden bowls by the man who cooked it, and he had to eat a little of each dish to show that there was no poison in it."

"Was there ever any poison?" I asked.

And she said, "No, no one ever tried to poison the king. Why should they? If there had been any of his brothers alive in the palace then no doubt attempts would have been made to poison the king. But they were all dead, Thakin, all but the two princes who had fled to Lower Burma. All was peace in the palace and in the kingdom."

They are very temperate people the Burmese, temperate in all ways, eating not very much ; you never see a gross fat man or woman in all the country, drinking not at all. There are stories amongst the English of how the king drank, and they are all untrue. My maid of honour laughed when I told them to her.

" Thakin," she said, " there was just a little story about the king when he first came to the throne, that he was so delighted at being king, so giddy at the sudden change that he hardly knew where he was. One evening he was led away by some of his pages and drank some beer, and disgraced himself. But he only did it once, and he was dreadfully ashamed of himself for long afterwards, that he had thus forgotten how a king should behave, that all the teaching of his days in the monastery were broken so quickly.

" The king was very much given to religion, Thakin, he was very fond of the sacred books and he often sent for the monks to come and teach him concerning all those things. And when the monk came the king would come down from his golden chair and sit on the floor with the pages and the monk would sit on the chair.

" He was fond of quoting from the sacred books,
and he was full of proverbs and wise sayings. I
think, Thakin, he would have done very well as a
monk, he would have been a very good man, a very
good man in a monastery where all temptation was
kept from him. But it is very hard to be a king.
When you have the power to do things, it is
very difficult not to do them. Every one liked the
king because he was good-natured and kind and
never wished to harm any one at all. Twice a day,
morning and evening, he would go to the pagoda
and repeat the teaching of the sacred books that he
had learnt in the monastery when he was a monk.
I suppose, Thakin, he would hardly realise them
then; but now that he is far away from all his people
a prisoner in a strange land he must understand,
'Trouble, weariness, illusion,' there is nothing in all
the world but that."

" Is that what they say at the pagoda when
they pray ? " I asked, and my maid of honour said,
" Yes, that is what they say."

For my maid of honour is religious; she too
goes to the pagoda often and to the rest-houses
to hear the law read and to fast on every Sun-
day. She has beads which she passes through
her slender fingers when she repeats her prayers.
She showed me hers once. They are just a

string of plain beads, not at all pretty nor ornamental.

"The queen," I asked, " did she too] go to the
pagoda ? "

"Yes, Thakin, she too would go twice a day,
at sunrise and sunset, to the pagoda, and she
would say as the king did, ' Trouble, weariness,
illusion,' and think of the teaching of the great
teacher."

"Is that all ?" I asked ; "would she not pray
for anything to be given her ? "

My maid of honour answered slowly, "How
should I know, Thakin ? The monks say there is no
prayer, that it is no good, that it is wrong. But
many women pray. Whom do they pray to ? I do
not know. Perhaps the Teacher may hear ; there in
the Great Peace, he may hear and understand and
help us who cry to him. What do they pray for ?
I think all women pray much the same. The
queen would ask that she might keep the love of
her husband and that her little son might not die.
A queen would not pray any different from other
women, Thakin, would she ? Her son died from
small-pox, and the Queen was very sorry. The
little girls did not die.

"They lived in a separate part of the palace,
and every morning they came to make their bows

to the king and queen—their father and mother. The girls lived, but the son died. And yet the queen did all she could to have strong children. When a baby was coming, she would eat lizard's eggs out of the jungle. They were toasted over a fire and are very strong food, and she would eat the flesh of unborn calves. Only she of all the people in the palace was allowed to eat beef, and then only when she was about to have a baby. But it was no good, the son died, Thakin. And the queen wanted a son to be king after her husband. Now I have heard that in that far place she has a son. I do not know if it be true, but if it be true, yet will he never be king after his father now."

That, my maid of honour told me, was the queen's greatest sorrow, that her son died ; and her great trouble, her great continued aim in life was to keep her husband true to her, to retain for herself the sole place in his affections. She tried every means to do this : by watching the king, by keeping temptation out of his way, and also, because she was without doubt a very clever woman, by making herself always pleasant and gracious to the king and by trying in all ways to retain her beauty. She was most careful about this my maid of honour says, careful to be always dressed in good taste, always neat, and with her face properly powdered and her hair beautifully arranged. She knew where the power of woman lies, and she did all she could to make herself attractive to the king. There was a European maid of honour in the palace, as I have said, and through this maid the queen obtained from Paris all the most famous cosmetiques to make her complexion clear and her lips red and her eyes bright, that she might be fair in his eyes. There was no one in the palace, says my maid of honour, like the queen, no one that had her grace and presence. " I do not know, Thakin, how the king could look on any one after the queen."

Yet he did. The Shan princess, if she was the first was not the last, and the next case did not end even so well as that.

It is a sad story, the story she told me of the king's next infidelity, full of pathos I think, it leaves one full of compassion for every one concerned : the king, and the girl, and the girl's people, but as much as any for the queen, one who felt herself disdained and plotted against, obliged to be on her guard and defend herself against all around her.

CHAPTER X

THE KING'S MISTRESS

It is the story of the Yenaung prince and the Kanni Wun's daughter, and this is how my maid of honour tells it.

"The Yenaung prince was not of royal birth at all. Who his people were I do not know, but they were not of great family or of any influence, and he became a prince all through the affection of the king. For when Prince Thibaw was a lad at school in the monastery the boy who was afterwards the Yenaung prince was at school with him, and they became friends. They must have had some tastes and desires in common one would suppose, but it is difficult to guess what they were, for in after life they differed as much as two men could differ. But they were friends, and although in those days there seemed to be no possibility that Prince Thibaw could come to be king yet his schoolfellow believed in him.

" 'You will be king one day,' said the boy to the prince. 'You will surely be king.'

" And when, as they were playing in the garden of the monastery, a kite swooped down and carried off the prince's turban the schoolfellow was even more certain.

" 'It is a sign,' he said, 'that you will be king.'

" The prince and the other boys laughed, but the boy was unmoved.

" 'You will surely be king. And promise me that when you are king you will not forget me, who am now telling you of what is to come.'

" The prince promised ; and when in the course of events the prophecy was fulfilled and the prince became king he did not forget. Thibaw as prince or as king never forgot his friends, and as soon as he was firmly on the throne he sent for the boy, who was now become a young monk, and raised him to the dignity of prince. All that the Yenaung prince asked the king gave : money and power and his affection, so that the Yenaung prince became almost a little king himself.

" King Thibaw loved him and the very poor people admired him because he was generous to them and gave away his money freely, but the better people disliked him and feared him, and the queen hated him above all.

" The better people feared him because he carried off their wives and daughters. Why the queen hated him will be seen later.

" He had many wives. It is impossible to say how many wives he had. Whenever he saw a nice-looking girl as he passed through the city he would send his followers to bring her to him, so that whenever it was feared he was about to ride through the city, all the pretty girls were hidden away by their parents lest they should be carried off.

" It was not necessary for the prince to see a girl before desiring her. If he only heard she was pretty that was sufficient : he must have her at once. And so men would come and tell him things out of spite. If a merchant had a beautiful daughter, wicked men would demand money from him, and if he would not pay, then they went and told the Yenaung prince that the girl was more beautiful than a fairy. The prince would immediately send off for her, and she would be torn from her home and given to the prince. No one could resist his force, for he had many armed men and was, moreover, the favourite of the king.

" The Yenaung prince lived there in his strong house with his many wives and his numerous followers. No one dared to try and interfere with him. He had electric bells fitted up from his room to the rooms of the wives, one bell to each, and when he wanted any particular wife he just touched her bell and she came running quickly. He did this so that the other wives should not know who was with him and be jealous. They only heard a bell ring somewhere, but they could not tell who it was the prince favoured. If he wanted them all he rang all the bells, and there was a noise as of a tempest of ringing, and girls came running from all their many rooms.

"The queen did not approve of this at all. She thought the Yenaung Prince was a wicked man living in such a scandalous way, and she had many complaints from parents about the carrying off of their daughters. The queen heard their complaints and she was very sorry, but she could do nothing.

"Often she spoke to the king about it, but without result.

"'What can I do?' the king would say; 'it is my brother's way. He has not got a wife like you, Su, Su'—so he always called the queen—'he has not got a wife like you. Perhaps he is trying to find one. When he does all this will stop. Shall we try and find one?'

"But the queen was not to be laughed off like this. She was very angry. She was scandalised at the prince's wickedness with women, and she feared the great escort of armed men he kept ready round his house. She feared too his influence upon the king, an influence that was always used against her.

" For the Yenaung prince used to laugh at the king because he was under the rule of the queen. He would jeer at the king, and the queen knew this and hated him in consequence.

" ' Where are the king's wives ? ' the Yenaung prince would ask. 'The king our father had fifty wives ; where are King Thibaw's wives ? Is it true they are locked up in prison ? '

" The king would look foolish at such questions, and then the Yenaung prince would tempt him to do as he did and have many mistresses. Gradually there grew up between the queen and the prince a deadly hatred and a knowledge that one of them must conquer the other, for that they could not continue like this. And so each sought whereby the other's influence might be destroyed.

" One day, about four years after he had come to the throne, King Thibaw went out of the palace to visit his brother the Yenaung prince. The king did not often go out of the palace, and then not very far, but sometimes he would go just as far as his brother's and stay there for a short time and talk, for he was very fond of the prince. And when they were alone there together in a room, the prince got up for a moment and presently returned with a girl, leading her by the hand. And the prince sat down again by the king and the girl knelt before them.

"The girl was very pretty, and she was confused and afraid to be brought thus before the king and she blushed, which made her more beautiful than before, and the king's eyes fell upon her with delight.

"'See now,' said the prince to the king, 'how beautiful she is : her eyes, how big they are, and her figure, how tall and slight. Is she not fit to be a queen ?'

"The king was delighted, and he fell in love with her as she sat there before him, and he said he had never seen any one so beautiful as she.

"'She is of good family,' said the prince ; 'her father is the Wun of Kanni, a powerful official and anxious to please the king. And the girl she is but seventeen years old, sweet as a champak bud, with a heart of gold.'

"Then seeing that the king's love was captured he went away out of the room leaving the king and the girl alone.

"The king was dreadfully in love with the girl. He loved her with all his soul and for a time he forgot the love of the queen. He forgot to love her, but he did not forget to fear her. What was he to do with this girl? He could not come often to the prince's house to meet her there, and if Mebya knew of her being introduced to the palace, there would be terrible trouble. What was to be done. The prince had a plan ready. The girl should accompany the king back to the palace dressed as a boy!"

This amongst the Burmans is quite easy. It meant just the change of a long silk instead of a skirt and a rearrangement of her hair. Girls and boys when they are under twenty are often so alike that one can easily pass for the other. It is quite a common ruse to dress one as the other. In a story I have to tell later on, it was a boy who was dressed as a girl and brought into the palace. In this case it was the girl who was to be dressed as a boy. And so in the Yenaung prince's house the girl was dressed up.

The flowers were taken from her hair and it was tied up like a man's, the powder was washed from her face and her necklaces and armlets were laid aside. A man's jacket was given to her and a man's long silk paso, while a sword was hung across her tender shoulders as if she were the follower of one of the court officials. And so dressed she was introduced quietly into the palace that evening and kept in a room on the pages' side of the palace, and no one knew. For the queen was sick, and her eye not so watchful as before.

How long she remained there unknown to all save a few I cannot say exactly, but it was several months. Of course it required time for the girl to consolidate her power over the king and for the plotters to find their opportunity. It was not intended that the girl should so remain for ever; some time she was to be queen. She was most carefully instructed by the Yenaung prince and her father of the game she was to play. She was to exert every nerve to bring the king entirely into her influence and to destroy that of the queen. She was so beautiful and so clever the plotters were sure she could do that. The plotters were also wide awake, strengthening their own influences and waiting on events, and they intended as soon as their plans were ripe to urge the king to dismiss the queen as the queen had herself dismissed her eldest sister, and place the Kanni Wun's daughter on the throne as queen.

It was a daring plot. It must have been nearly

successful for the girl to have been there so long and undiscovered. For the palace was full of prying eyes that saw, full of listening ears that heard all that went on ; full of secret tongues that told the queen all that she might desire to learn. And yet for months she did not know.

The girl lived there disguised as a page, hidden in the men's part of the palace, and the king met her daily, sometimes here and sometimes there, where no one could disturb them, and the queen did not know.

How it all came out I do not know, but suddenly it was all discovered.

My maid of honour gave a scornful little laugh when she told me.

" They were very clever ; they thought themselves so very clever and that they could deceive the queen and dethrone her. As if their little minds could plot against the queen whose mind was greater than any one's in the kingdom.

" For a time they were successful, but at last the queen found it all out. And in a thought, in a moment, before the king had even time to realise that he was discovered, before the girl and her people had time to attempt to escape, the girl and her father and all those who had taken part in the plot were seized and executed.

" Thakin, it was a terrible time.   The queen was
like a mad thing, when she saw how very nearly
she had been to losing the king and all that made
her life worth living.

" She had forgiven the Shan princess, but there
could be no more forgiveness.   Moreover she was
older now and stronger and her power was
established.   All those who plotted against her
must understand that they staked their lives on
their plots.   There were many people in this plot—
all who could be found were executed."

" And the king ?" I asked.   " He was king.
Could he not save his mistress and those who had
helped him ?   Was he quite helpless ? "

" Ah ! Thakin, you do not understand.   If you
had ever seen the queen you would not ask that.
No one could stand against her when she was
angry.   Not the ministers, nor the king, nor any
one.   It were better to face a tigress.   Every one
bent and shivered before her, and whatever orders
she gave were carried out.   The king was but a
foolish school-boy before her.   When the queen
was angry she was queen and king too, and there
was no one beside her in power.

" She was dreadfully angry.   No words can
say how angry she was at being disdained and
plotted against by little people, at having the

king's affections stolen from her. She was fighting for her life, for what was more than life to her.

"People say she was cruel and vindictive, but she was only cruel to those who plotted against her.

"And so the girl, the beautiful young girl, with the big eyes and the skin like gold, was executed, and all her relations.

"Of all those in the plot but two remained—the king and the Yenaung prince."

It must be remembered, when considering the king's part in all this, that he was entitled by all law, by all custom, to have four chief queens. His father, King Mindon, the great king, had done so—all kings of Burma had done so.

That he should take to himself the Kanni Wun's daughter to be a queen was not considered disgraceful, but, on the contrary, honourable and right. To all the men of the old school the king's subservience to one wife was considered weak and contemptible. All the influence of the whole palace, of the queen-mother, of the ministers, of all the *entourage* of the throne was lent to induce the king to take other wives. Perhaps thereby the ascendency of the queen might be destroyed and the petticoat government overthrown. The king was within his rights in all he did, and the catastrophe is but a proof of the extraordinary ascendency this girl queen had obtained over every one.

Custom and tradition, influence of ministers, the opinion of the nations were nothing to her. She threw all these things to the winds, and no one could stand before her.

CHAPTER XI

THE DEATH OF THE YENAUNG PRINCE

ONCE more was the queen again queen. She had overthrown her enemies and her rivals, and she stood supreme in all the palace, in all the kingdom. No one was so great as she, because she held the king in the palm of her hand and could do unto him as she would. All her enemies had fallen ; all who were concerned in bringing the Kanni Wun's daughter into the palace were dead, save one.

The Yenaung prince was still there. Though the queen could kill many people yet could she not kill him. He was brother to the king, and was safe. The king loved him as he had always done, and before long would listen to him again. When the queen frowned at the prince and refused to receive him he only laughed. She could not hurt him.

Then a strange thing happened.

It was a custom always of the Burmese kings to

have four great chests placed in various quarters of the city. They were made of teak, very strong, with gold mouldings upon them and a heavy lock to fasten them. At the top was a slit, and when people wished to petition the king and could not gain access to the palace to present their petitions, they put them in one of these boxes. They were brought every day to the palace to the king, and the queen opened them with the keys, and the letters and petitions were read by the queen, who showed them to the king.

"Thus the king came to hear of many things that would not otherwise have reached his ears. All sorts of letters were put in the boxes—complaints against officials for dishonesty and cruelty, petitions for justice and for the king's favour, accusations against high ministers. Any one who had a hatred towards an official wrote a petition secretly and put it in the box, and so it came to the king. Many of these were never signed with any name, were but stings in the dark, and some were untrue, but often these boxes were the means of discovering great frauds and great injustice and putting them right. The king never did anything merely on the letters themselves, but when an accusation was made he appointed a minister to inquire into the case and see if it were true. If it were, he punished the culprit;

if not, he tried to find out who wrote the letter so as to punish him.

"Now, about this time the boxes came to be full of accusations against the Yenaung prince. He was plotting against the king, so the letters said. He wanted to be king himself. He declared openly that King Thibaw was only a puppet ruled by a woman, unfit to be the king of a great nation. King Thibaw, he said, knew nothing of the world, while he, the prince, knew a great deal. The king was cooped up in his palace under the command of a girl, but the prince went about, and the people knew him, and the soldiers liked him. So ran these unsigned petitions.

"Every day they came in, every day fresh proofs were offered of the truth of these accusations. The prince was collecting men. He had a little army at his house, he had many more up and down the kingdom. He knew also how to lead` fighting men, while the king was but a monk let loose.

"These things went to the king's heart because many of them were true. The prince had a great following. He knew that, and the prince knew how to manage his men, while he the king knew nothing. If it came to a fight the prince would have the advantage. Then, many of the ministers were angry with the king, and more especially with the queen. The Kanni Wun had many relations and friends, and all these were alarmed at the way the king had allowed the queen to execute the Wun and girl. Many people were disgusted at it all.

" So when the warnings came thicker and thicker every day the king began to believe them and to be much afraid. He caused inquiries to be made and these seemed to support the letters. It was true that the prince was very angry with the king about the Wun's daughter. It is true that many officials went to see the prince. It was true that he had a great following of armed men. Therefore the king soon believed that it was true that the prince intended to depose him and execute him and the queen.

" He was terribly frightened. How much of all this was really true I cannot say. People who ought to know declare the prince never had any idea of dethroning his brother. They say that these letters and warnings were all sent by the queen, all a plot of hers to cause the destruction of her enemy the prince. Who shall say ? The lives of kings and princes are full of terrors ; it is easy to make a king believe that there is a plot against him even if it be not true. There are so many true plots that no king can afford to disregard what he hears, even if he is not sure. A mistake, too much confidence, means fall and death. So the king believed.

"After the execution of the Wun's daughter, for some time the king had not seen the prince. The king was very much ashamed and the prince was very angry. Perhaps it was the king's shame that made him quicker to think evil of his brother.

" Then one day the king sent for the prince. He sent a pleasant message that it was a long time since he had seen his brother and would he come to the palace, for there was something the king wished to say to him.

"The message was pleasant and the prince suspected nothing. He had no idea that the king had been told that he, the prince, was plotting against him. He had no idea there was anything in the wind but just a little talk. Had he guessed he would never have gone. But he guessed nothing and he went.

" He came to where the king was sitting with the queen in their rooms near the portico, and he bowed down on his face before the king as is the court custom.

" And as he bowed, the king drew forth from his sheath the short sword that he always wore and held it over the prince, his face full of anger.

' You deserve,' he said, ' that I should kill you as you sit ; you have been plotting to kill me. What can you say to save your life ? '

" The prince was very much surprised, very much afraid, but for a time he said nothing, and the king remained there with his drawn sword over the prince, the blade shaking with the anger that was in the king. All those who were about were terribly afraid and very sorry for the prince, fearing what would come next, all but the queen. She was not sorry, nor afraid, but she looked at the prince kneeling there in peril of his life and she smiled and smiled, but between her parted lips were her teeth tight closed.

" ' What have you to say,' said the king, ' you, whom I have loved as my own brother, you who have plotted to kill me ? What have you to say ? '

" And the prince answered that he had nothing to say. ' If you want to kill me, kill,' he said.

" And so because he was too proud to answer, the king ceased to question him and he was given to the guards and led away to prison.

Then were messengers sent to the prince's house to search it for proof of his guilt. They found there what was they said certain proof. In his bedroom there was a great golden bed, and that bed was made in a fashion that only kings are allowed to use. So there was no doubt about the prince's guilt. He was plotting to be king and was in his heart king already. In public he was prince, but in private, to his wives and to himself, he was king.

"The report was brought back to the palace and told to the king, and he believed. He was very angry with the prince his brother, and he left him there in the prison till he thought how he must be dealt with. He must consider what could be done with the prince his brother.

"The queen watched the king's face to know what he would do; she watched and waited. When the prince was arrested the queen was glad, and when the news of his royal bed was brought she was still more pleased. For the king's face became clouded and he was angry.

"But when the next day the king's face began to lighten, the queen became anxious. She watched and watched, and she saw at length the king's gentle-heartedness, his love for his brother, coming back, and all the anger fading away from his eyes. He began to be sorry for his brother and to think of him, and he ceased to talk to the queen as they were sitting together and to answer to her questions. Each day after the prince's arrest the king seemed to be drifting away from the queen.

"All the whole palace witnessed it, and we were sure that before many days the king would forgive the prince and restore him to honour as before.

"And then," says my maid of honour, "one day the queen gave news to the king. It was in the little garden pavilion early in the morning, and the king and queen sate there and listened to the birds who called from bush to bush through all the scented groves. They were very fond of sitting there just by themselves while the princesses and the maids of honour walked down below or played in the gardens round about. No one would be near only I, who rolled the cigarettes for the queen, and a girl who fanned her.

"The king and queen sat and they said nothing. The king's eyes were far away watching the purple shadows on the far-off mountains to the east, sitting very quietly. The queen made one or two remarks to him, but he did not reply, only looked and looked at the far-off hills. And the queen watched his face, trying to see what was on his mind.

"The cries of the girls running in the gardens came to us, broken by the trees, and gongs rang now and then in the palace grounds.

" The queen turned suddenly to the king.

" ' Maung, Maung,' she said, ' what are you thinking of ? '

" The king nodded towards the far-off hills. ' See how cool they look,' said the king, ' and how fresh, while here it is so hot.'

" The queen looked at the hills. ' Yes,' she said, ' from far away they look beautiful, but if you come near who can tell ? Perhaps they are not so.'

" ' Behind these hills,' continued the king, ' is my own city, the one from which I was named, the city of Thibaw. But I have never been there. Some day we will go, Su, Su, to see it.

" ' Yes,' said the queen, ' when there is no more trouble. When the country is quiet, and there is no one to plot, then will we go.'

" ' You and I, Su, Su,' said the king, smiling at her, ' and my brother the Yenaung prince. You will be friends with him then again, and all of us will go together.'

" But at the prince's name the queen's face grew angry. Her eyes shone out from under her drawn-down brows as she turned upon the king.

" ' Never will you go with the Yenaung prince,' she said sharply. ' Never will you see him again. For he is dead.'

" The king turned with frightened face to the queen and put his hand upon her shoulders.

" ' What is that you say, Su, Su ? '

" The queen shook off his hand. 'Oh,' she said, ' did you not know ? Where are your ministers not to tell you ? I thought of course that you knew. He died of fever last night.'

" The king looked at the queen and his face became full of sorrow, and tears came into his eyes. ' My brother,' he said, ' my brother,' and as he looked reproach came into his look, reproach of the queen and a question that he dared not ask.

" But the queen stared back at the king, her face like iron, and at length the king's eyes fell before hers.

" ' I am very glad,' said the queen slowly. ' I am glad that he is dead.'

" At her words certainty came to the king. He knew then of what sort of fever his brother had died.

" Without a word he rose. Without a word or sign he came down from the summer-house, and went away walking very slowly towards the palace and went up the steps towards his own rooms. He called to a page as he went to fetch a secretary, and then the doors shut and the king was lost to sight.

"But the queen never moved. Her face was quite white and her breath came quickly as if she had been running in a race, and had won.

"Down below the girls ran to and fro in the gardens and splashed the waters, and the sounds came more clearly because of the stillness in the pavilion.

"Then at length she too went away. But she did not follow the king to his rooms as she went, but went now to the north of the palace till she came to where her mother lived in the rooms by the little golden spire. Here she went in leaving us without.

"Not all the rest of that day did she see the king, for he kept to his own rooms.

"So did the queen give the news to the king of the death of her last enemy."

CHAPTER XII

THE QUEEN'S SELF-JUSTIFICATION

" It was a day or two after the Yenaung prince died," said my maid of honour, " and it was very hot in the palace. Outside the sun was blazing down making the golden *façades* one great stream of flame. And in the gardens the air was hushed in heat ; the leaves hung motionless upon the trees, and the shadows lay as pools in the grass. All the birds were still, except the crows, who panted with red, opened beaks and cawed hoarsely now and again.

" Inside the palace it was as silent as without. The great state chambers were vacant. The queen had retired to her private apartments to sleep, the king was away no one knew where. A few days before the queen would never have allowed the king to go away from her, but now that the Yenaung prince was dead there was no one to fear, and she could go and sleep in peace. Four or five girls were with the queen fanning her, and awaiting her waking, but the rest of us were in our great room where we stayed while on duty on the queen.

"It was so hot there, Thakin—you know how hot it can be sometimes just before a storm comes. It was so hot we did not know what to do. The great doors that gave upon the courtyard near the fountain were wide open. For no man dared to come that side of the palace. The approaches were all guarded by armed soldiers to keep intruders from the places of the queen. And so, Thakin, although the doors were widely opened so that any breeze might come in the girls were not afraid. Here and there they sat about on cushions or mats upon the floor, reading, talking, sleeping. Many had taken off their jackets that were tight and hot, and just tossed a corner of their satin kerchiefs across their bosoms. They were so pretty, Thakin, ah, so pretty as they lay about in their silken dresses with soft, fair arms and shoulders against the gold and crimson of the walls.

"I was sitting away in a dark cool corner of the great room with another girl, my friend Ma Shwe Lon, and we talked to each other in little whispers about all that had happened in the last few days. We were only children in that far-away time, but

children in a palace grow quickly and see much.
And so we talked of the Yenaung prince and how
he had died and how glad we all were. For the
Yenaung prince had been to us a threat and fear.
We knew he hated the queen and would try to get
her into trouble, and we loved the queen and hated
the prince. So we were glad that the prince was
gone. It was to us as the lifting of a great cloud,
the passing of a terrible fear. For days and days
we had hardly dared to laugh or talk or play for
the fear that hung over us. But now all was safe
again. Such a change no one can imagine it.

"But although we were all pleased, we knew
that many people were angry. The king was sad,
and several ministers were angry and afraid, and
many of the common people were angry. For the
devil prince had been generous with the money
the king gave him, and threw it to the people, and
he went often abroad in state for the people to see
him, so that he was popular in a way amongst the
common folk. Many of them would be sorry at
his death.

We talked to each other about this.

"Presently we noticed coming across the sun-
drowned courtyard two ladies. They came to our
room and the head of our company of maids of
honour went to speak to them, and they sat down.

We were curious to know who they were and so we crept quite near and hid behind a great golden pillar and looked at them.

"One of them we recognised at once as the wife of one of the secretaries of the palace. She had been a maid of honour before she was married to the secretary, and we knew her quite well.

"But the other girl was a stranger. She was very pretty. Of all the girls that I have seen none have been prettier than this girl. She was tall and rather slender and her hands were so tiny and so fair. Her cheeks were round and soft, with little dimples in them when she smiled. Her eyes were big and lustrous, like those of the deer that live by the feet of the great hills, and her voice had a ripple in it as of water falling far away. No one could see her and not love her, but she seemed a little sad, as if some trouble had come to her and she was afraid. She sat leaning upon a cushion, and she kept her face to the ground and only spoke in little words when she was addressed. She was come by the queen's order, so we guessed, but for what reason we could not tell. Only the chief maid of honour said to her, 'Sit down here, Ma Le, and wait. Before long the queen will awake and will send for you. And do not be afraid before the queen. Be sure that the queen will not wish to hurt you. So be of good courage, and when the queen speaks to you answer clearly.'

"When I heard the chief maid of honour call her Ma Le, and when I looked carefully at her, I remembered who she was. For I had known her a little when I was able to leave the palace and go to see my mother in the city.

"She had lived not very far from us. I had not seen her for a long time and she seemed changed, so that was why I did not recognise her at once. But when I remembered who she was, I looked round the pillar at her and nodded and smiled. And she, when she saw me, nodded and smiled too with surprise at seeing me there. I could not go and speak to her then as I was afraid of the chief maid of honour, so I went away back to my dark corner, and sat and wondered why Ma Le had come to the palace, and what the queen wanted to say to her, and why she looked sad. But I could not think of anything.

"Presently the queen's gong rang, the clear silver gong that warned us the queen was risen. All of us were awake at once. You saw the girls who were lying asleep jump up in a hurry and those who were talking stop in the middle of a sentence. There was no delay allowed when the queen called. We put on our jackets in a great hurry, and one girl said to another, 'Tell me now if my hair is straight?' 'Are my flowers right?' 'Is the powder on my face smudged?' Such a hurrying there was and looking in mirrors and straightening of dresses.

"Then we went out across the courtyard to the great glass chamber with the daïs at one end. All the room was covered with glass. There were glass crystals on the pillars, and glass panels on the walls containing flowers, and the ceiling was gold. In front, the room was open, the walls lifting up, and there was the garden where the birds were beginning to awake and the flowers to raise their heads as the cool fresh evening breeze came wandering over them.

The queen was not in the room when we arrived, and so we went and sat in our places at the back of the daïs, and Ma Le with the lady who came with her knelt in front awaiting the queen. Presently ` the queen came in with the king. They came hand-in-hand as they went always, and their cushions were placed for them and they sat down on the daïs. The king was sad and troubled, but the queen was fresh from her sleep, and laughed like a girl who is free from care, for she was but a girl, Thakin; even when the palace fell she was only a girl still.

"The queen looked round upon us all and smiled. She liked to see us look pretty and happy ; we were her own maids of honour, and she cared for us as if we had been her sisters. And then she looked at Ma Le kneeling before the daïs very much afraid, and her brows came together and she asked, ' Who is this? Is this the girl whom the Yenaung prince stole ? ' The lady with her said, ' Yes.'

"The pleasure was gone from the queen's eyes, the ripple that danced within them was dead, and we could see the anger in them deep down, like a flame in the dark.

"' This is,' said the queen, 'the girl whom the prince stole. One of many whom he stole.' She spoke very slowly in her clear voice, clearer than any gong.

"' Tell me, now,' said the queen to Ma Le, ' tell to the king, and to me, and to the princesses and the maids of honour, who you are, and what it is that has happened to you. For we would hear what you have suffered at that prince's hands.'

"The queen ceased, and we all kept very quiet, looking at Ma Le, waiting for her to speak. But she was so afraid that she could not. Her shoulders trembled as she knelt, and her face was hidden in her hands.

"Then after a minute the queen spoke very softly.

' Do not be afraid,' she said. 'There is no one here but who will be kind to you. Are we not women and can understand ? '

" But Ma Le was still very much afraid and her voice was full of tremble, and she began to speak, and stopped, and so I crept from where I was very quietly, and I came to her and knelt by her and took her hand.

" I felt so sorry for her kneeling there, and she was so pretty. It did not seem as if she was the grown-up woman and I the little girl, but as if I was her big friend who ought to encourage her.

" ' Do not be afraid,' I whispered to her.

" The queen laughed and said, ' See now this very little maid is not afraid. You are a big woman, so be not so frightened.'

" Then at last Ma Le began to speak. At first she spoke so low that the queen had to bend forward to listen, but after a little she got more courage.

" She told of who she was, how her father had been a goldsmith in the city, and how her mother had died when she was a little girl, and she had lived alone with her father all her childhood. And how when she was grown up to be a big girl she was married to her husband, who was an officer in one of the king's regiments of horse. Her husband came to her father's house and they all lived there together in such happiness as could never be forgotten.

"Her father worked at his work, making gold ornaments and silver bowls for the ministers and the rich people of the palace, and her husband went about his duties each day with his soldiers, returning every evening to his wife who was waiting for him. Never was there any trouble or any sorrow in that house. Then it happened that one day, in the middle of the day, when it was very hot, Ma Le was asleep. She had been up very early in the morning seeing to her husband's wants and the household requirements, and so she was tired and she went to sleep. And in her sleep there came to her a great noise from outside, the sound of men shouting and the trampling of horses, the rustle and movement of people.

"So, startled and not knowing what it could be, she ran out into the verandah and looked.

"It was the Yenaung prince passing by. With a great concourse of soldiers and servants, some in front of him clearing the way, and others following behind, he came riding along on his pony. Many of the people in the streets had run away down bye-streets or into houses to get away from the men with the sticks, and those who could not so escape were kneeling by the side of the road, and bowed to the prince as he passed.

" And as Ma Le came running into the verandah her face flushed with sleep and her hair all ruffled the prince passed just under the verandah.

" When Ma Le saw who it was she ran away within and hid. But it was too late. For the prince had seen her.

"Then she told the queen of how terrified she was, and how she had told her father and her husband when he came home and how for days they lived in terror. And then one day her husband was sent for by the commandant of his regiment and never returned, not though his wife waited up all the night did he come back to her.

" But there came instead men from the Yenaung prince and they caught her and put her on an elephant and carried her away to his house. Although she cried yet it was of no use. Even as she now recalled it all tears came into her eyes, though she sate before the queen.

" She told of how she was received into the prince's house and how many women there were there, and how she was taught to dance and made to perform before the prince, as if she had been but a dancing girl. Herewith she said things of what had happened in the prince's house, things

that made the queen's brows come lower and lower
and even the king looked ashamed. Of how many
men were killed in that house and how the prince
was said to eat men's flesh and to live as if he
were lower than any beast.

"There she lived many, many months until at last
the prince was dead and she was free.

"'But now,' said Ma Le, 'though I am free
what is the use of it? For my father is dead with
shame and my husband no one can tell what has
become of him. Surely he is dead too. And if
he were not, who am I now to be his wife, I that
have been mistress to another man and made to
dance like a dancing girl? Surely it was better that
I too were dead with them.'

"So Ma Le told her story, and as she finished her
eyes were full of tears and her throat of sobs for
her father and for her husband and for herself.
Many of the maids of honour too were full of
sorrow for this girl and they looked sad, but in the
queen's face there was both sorrow and great
anger. There was compassion for those who had
suffered, anger for him who had caused it, and
she turned and looked at the king to see what he
thought.

"But the king looked away. He was angry still
with the queen for the prince's death and even

though he was sorry for Ma Le yet would he not show that he was angry with what his brother had done.

" So the queen turned away from the king and looked upon the princesses and the maids of honour and those who were in attendance, and she spoke :

" 'You have all heard,' said the queen, ' this story that the girl has told us. It is a truth that should be carefully considered. For she is not a common girl but of respectable people.

" 'Her father was a goldsmith and made no doubt many of the gold things we have here. He was an honest man. And her husband was an officer in the king's cavalry. But the prince did not care for any of these things. Because he liked her pretty face he cared not what trouble he brought upon her and her husband. Surely even tigers are not so bad. Think now,' she went on to her maids of ' honour, ' suppose this girl were you or your sister or that her husband were your brother. Then will you understand how vile were the deeds of this prince.' She paused a moment and all of us were silent with fear and sorrow, no one even moved.

" For the queen's eyes blazed and her golden bracelets trembled on her wrists and her face was white. She was terrible to look at.

"'Such,' she repeated very low and clearly, 'was the prince, a dishonourer of women, a murderer of men. Is it not right for all men to rejoice that he is dead?'

"She looked round upon the king, but he never moved, he looked away as if not hearing, as if it were some private business of the queen that was not for him. There was a long, long silence. Outside you heard the birds twitter to each other in the gardens and the soft sweet murmur of the breeze among the trees.

" A distant gong sounded in the guard.

" Thakin, this was the defence of the queen, her justification before the king and people for the execution of the Yenaung prince. For she knew that the whole kingdom would talk about it, that many people that did not know would perhaps condemn her because of her having him executed. And so she had called Ma Le and made her tell her story there before all of us that we might understand. And she knew that we would tell our relations and friends till many heard of it.

" Was there ever a woman so clever as our queen?"

CHAPTER XIII

ROYAL COOKERY

It was in February 1884 that the Yenaung prince
was executed. The five years that the queen had
sat upon the throne had changed her from a child
to a woman, had given into her hands all the power
and the authority of the kingdom. When in the
early days of her reign the Shan princess offended
her, she was expelled from the palace, but when,
later, the Kanni Wun's daughter attempted to usurp
her authority, the answer was death.

Five years of incessant watchfulness, of constant
danger, had turned this unformed girl into a re-
morseless queen. She had learnt to fight and to
win, and to show no mercy to the vanquished.

But in other ways she seems to have changed
but little, to have hardly grown older at all.

All the great world was hidden from her and her
husband. They lived within these palace walls
shut in from all tha tmatures the understanding; of

all that went on without they were hopelessly ignorant. They did not know, and I do not think they very much cared. As long as the queen could keep the king to herself she was satisfied and happy. That was all the wisdom she wished to have.

The king's desire was for a quiet life. If only there could be peace, and people would give up scheming and plotting, quarrelling and fighting, all would be well. As for political affairs, had they not ministers?

So in the intervals between the plots and the assassinations they played. They ran about the gardens and hid in the thickets, and laughed with the abandon of children.

"Thakin," said my maid of honour, "did you ever hear of a king and queen cooking their own dinner?"

I said that none of the kings and queens of my acquaintance would do such a thing.

"No," she acquiesced. "It is quite unheard of. But my king and queen did so one day."

"What for?" I asked.

"For fun. There was nothing to do one afternoon. It was hot, and we were all sleepy except the queen. She was not sleepy at all. Suddenly she said to the king, 'There is nothing to do, let us cook our own dinner. I never cooked a dinner, did you?' The king said he never did. The queen said it was a thing everybody ought to know, even kings, and it must be great fun.

"We were sent off in a hurry. Some went to get firewood, others to get earthenware pans for cooking, others for rice and water. It was, 'A hundred rupees for a pumpkin,' or 'Here, five hundred rupees for some curry powder,' or 'A thousand rupees for a few chillies.'

"We got all the things at last, and put them down in the shade outside in the garden, and the king and queen set to work. They should not let any one help. So we sat around and looked on.

"The king lit the fire after much trouble, and made himself dreadfully dirty doing it. One of us had to tell him how to do it, and how to put three bricks to hold up the pots.

"The queen put the rice into the cooking-pot with water. She ought to have washed the rice first, but she did not know that. Then the king set to and made another fire between three bricks and boiled the rice while the queen made the curry. She did not know anything about making curries, and she kept asking questions all the time. She never peeled the pumpkin, and she put in far too much chillies.

"While the king and queen were arguing how much salt there ought to be in the curry, the fire under the rice went out, and the king had to light it again. When he thought the rice was sufficiently cooked he took it off, and thought that all was done. But he could not understand why it was so wet. We had to tell him to pour off the water and dry the rice over the fire, stirring it about.

"When at last it was done we had all of us to eat it, for the queen said she was not hungry. She ate just a little, and we had to eat the rest. It was not good at all. The rice was quite hard in the middle, not sufficiently cooked, and it was smoky, too, and the curry was so hot that tears came into our eyes.

"Fortunately there were a great many of us, and every one wanted to eat a little because the king and queen had cooked it. For no one had ever before heard of a king and queen cooking their dinner. It was a quite unknown thing in all the world for kings and queens to cook. But it was very amusing.

"For three or four days after that the king and queen cooked their dinner every day, and they got to know how to do it quite well at last. The king could boil rice just as well as any one after a little practice, and the queen even learnt how to make cakes like the Japanese woman. Then they got tired of it, and did not cook again. But it was very great fun while it lasted. Ah, Thakin, it was pleasant in the palace in those days."

And as she talked there came into my mind a saying of the wise old minister the Kinwun Mingyi in these last days of the fall. Now one day he went into the palace to see the king about some very important business, that business on which lay the fate of the king and queen and their followers and people, and he could get no attention because the king was playing with the queen. The minister went away sadly to face the ruin coming swiftly up the river, and when he came without the palace to his own house he met there some of his advisers, Europeans who were trying to help him to save the king in spite of the king. They asked him how he had sped in his interview, and the minister told them what had happened—how the king was at play and could not be disturbed. " The kingdom," he said, "is in the hands of children. There is no hope at all."

Yes, they were only children ; full of impulses like children ; impulses towards good, towards evil, with no very settled purpose towards anything. They would make up their minds one day to one thing and the next to another. They were without the knowledge that alone could have directed their paths. And I do not think their councillors were much better than they—in knowledge I mean. True there was the Kinwun Mingyi, the wise old minister, the favourite of the late king. But he was only one, and often he was not listened to at all, and sometimes perhaps his advice was not good.

They were full of impulses, as I have said, eagerly desiring one thing to-day and forgetting it to-morrow. The king desired to have an army modelled upon European designs, armed with European arms, fit to fight for the kingdom when in danger. And so with great difficulty he obtained arms, cannons and rifles, and European instructors to drill his men in their uses. But when these European instructors took their troops out to the country behind Mandalay to practise those arms, to learn how to shoot and drill, there was a terrible commotion. The noise of the firing was heard in the palace and caused great consternation. No one knew what it could be : was it a Chinese army attacking Mandalay or a rebellion or what ? There was a panic in the city, and the bazaars closed, women shrieked and men hid their valuables as in time of war.

When the mounted men who were sent speeding

in all directions for news came and reported that it was only the European officer drilling his troops the fear turned into anger.

Urgent orders were sent to him to desist at once and never on any future occasion to behave in this way again. Hints, pretty broad hints, were thrown out as to what the consequences would be. And so, though the troops were armed and partly drilled, there the matter ended. The artillery could not be practised, the infantry could not become marksmen. Their weapons remained to them but ornamental appendages, rather heavy and useless than formidable. Such was the army of the king. This was an example of many things.

It occurred to the queen once that it would be a good idea to send some little girls to be educated in European fashion. As the king had sent some pages to France to learn something of the wisdom of the west, so she the queen would send some maids of honour to be brought up as European girls are brought up. They would on their return lend an additional lustre to her court, and be able to teach the other maids useful things, and be besides able to amuse the queen in the evening with stories of their adventures.

Four little girls were chosen, and were put under the care of the Roman Catholic sister in the palace, to be taken away and brought up in western ideas.

" She took them away," said my maid of honour, " and kept them for a year or two and took them to Bengal and elsewhere, I think, and after a time they came back again to Mandalay, and the queen sent for them to come to her in the palace, and they came.

" They were dressed in European dress, and their hair was done in European fashion, and, ah, Thakin! you have no idea how ugly they looked. Amid all the bright dresses of the maids of honour with their silk skirts and pure white jackets they looked as sombre as crows. English girls look nice in English dress, but Burmese girls look dreadful. I never saw any Burmese girls in English dress since, and I never want to. They looked so common. Yet they were pretty little girls. They wore their hair down their backs loose, which did not seem to us at all proper.

"They had lost all their manners. They did not know what to do. They came into the queen's presence and stood up before her not knowing what to do. Everybody must sit down before the queen, but these children had not as much manners or sense as the fish in the water-tanks.

" The queen looked at them for a moment,

and it was easy to see that she was not at all pleased.

"'Sit down,' she said, but they did not move. They were frightened, I think, and did not understand, only looked about foolishly. The queen caught one by the wrist and pulled her down, and then the others sat down. The queen then looked at them all over and said at last, 'They are very ugly. I do not think much of the European dress, why, it makes their faces look quite black.' And so it did, Thakin, much darker than if they wore our dress.

"Then the queen asked them what they had learnt and they could not say.

"'Can you speak any foreign languages?' she asked, and they said, 'Yes.'

"'Then say some,' said the queen.

"The children were afraid, and at first did not know what to say. At last one of them said something. I think the language was French, not the same as the Thakin speaks.

"The queen listened and shook her head. 'There has been a lot of money spent on those children,' she said, 'but I do not see much good of it. They have become ugly and very morose.' Then she noticed that one had a chain round her neck. 'What is this?' she said, and pulled it. The chain came out and with it a little image at the end. 'What is that image?' she asked, and the little girl said it was the image of God.

"The queen was scandalised. 'I sent you away,' she said, 'to learn the customs of the west and you come back looking very ugly, with no manners and very stupid. And you carry the image of a foreign idol about your neck. Take them away,' she said to us, 'take them away and dress them properly and teach them manners and remove their idols.'

"Mebya was not at all pleased with these children, Thakin, and indeed I do not think any one thought much of them, but soon they became like every one else."

Thus ended the queen's attempt at introducing western cultivation among her maids, so ended the king's attempts after western discipline for his troops. For they had no real knowledge of the world at all. They had no one to help them to it, and what little half knowledge there was that penetrated the palace, reached them in an unpleasant form.

I think it would be difficult to exaggerate the ignorance of these children, not only of the western world but even of their own country and their own people. They hardly ever went out of the palace, and when they did it was a ceremonious procession. Truth could not come to them save through a hundred filters that took from it all that was valuable, deprived it of all usefulness. Newspapers were of course unknown in Upper Burma and those from Lower Burma never reached there.

I asked my maid of honour once if they ever saw newspapers or news-letters of any kind in the palace.

"No," she said, "there were no newspapers in the palace. Besides, what is the good of them? There are newspapers now and I have once or twice read the *Mandalay Times*, which I have seen at my mother's house. It says that a man fell down out of a house somewhere and broke his neck. And that the Japanese are taking some place I never heard of before, and that some great ship has sunk near Belat. I do not care to know these things. What is the use of them even if they are true? And I do not know if they are true. I have a cousin who helps in one of the papers and he tells me that many of the things are not true at all. I do not see the use of papers."

"They are not any use," I answered, "except to the proprietors. I suppose your cousin gets paid for his work."

"Little enough," she answered. "Besides, it is

a great shame to make money by selling things that are all made up. I do not think government ought to allow newspapers. Besides, they are very rude sometimes."

So I suppose they have been making disagreeable remarks about some of her friends, but she did not tell me what they were.

And so these children the king and queen lived in the palace, not knowing very much, not caring perhaps very much, and the country was left a prey to governors and ministers and officials, the greatest surely of all the five evils.

The king was full of good intentions, hopelessly ignorant of how to carry them out, and the queen was full of good intentions too. Within her little circle of knowledge she did what she thought was the best always. She had rigid ideas of conjugal fidelity. As she would allow the king no other mistress, so it was with all her people. Any complaint to her by a wronged woman was sure to receive immediate notice.

No woman was allowed to be wrongfully divorced, to be abandoned, to be badly treated, in her times. She inaugurated amid her followers an ideal of domestic faith, new and unknown to the palace people, though not of course to the people at large.

The courtiers had followed the morals of their king, but now they were to be taught to follow the morals of their queen. For all her sex, in palace and city, she was a sure refuge in time of trouble. Any sketch of the queen would be imperfect if this were not fully explained and insisted upon. Her reign was to be a reign of·virtue if she could so make it. Her punishments for any breach were terribly severe. She was like all women, cruel and vindictive when she thought her rights were assailed, her orders disobeyed.

Her severity extended even unto her own house. There were to be no exceptions to the laws of virtue.

CHAPTER XIV

A PRINCESS AND HER LOVER

" THERE was a princess, a half sister to the king and queen, younger than he, younger than Mebya, one of the youngest of all the princesses. She had a household of her own, as had all the princesses, with rooms of her own apart and attendants of her own. She was very pretty too, as were most of the princesses, and she was religious. She was very fond of telling her beads before the pagoda in the palace, very fond of reading in the sacred books, very fond of going with her attendants to the monastery outside the palace near the south wall, to give offerings to the monks and hear them preach.

" Almost every full moon day and new moon day, and the days half way between, would she go early to the rest house by this monastery to sit all day in meditation on the sacred teaching, to eat but one meal before noon, to hear the monks read the sacred books. And so it happened that one evening in the rest house she noticed behind the monk who was reading, attending on him, a boy. All boys must, as the Thakin knows, enter into a monastery once in their lives, be accepted into the monkhood, wear the yellow robe and live the holy life if it be only for the months of fasting. No man is a proper Buddhist until he has done this. And the boy had just taken the vows of the monkhood, just shaved his head and taken on him the yellow robe, and he sat behind his teacher holding his fan with downcast eyes as monks should.

"When the princess saw him she thought he was the most loveable of all boys that she had seen. She could not speak to him of course.

"He was there a monk with the monks, and they may only speak to a woman in company and in an open space. But she could go often to the monastery to give offerings and hope to see the little novice. If she was religious before, she was far more so now. She was always coming to the monastery, always giving presents, till even the monks wondered. Sometimes when she came she would see the boy, but often he was with his teacher and did not appear, and even when she saw him it was from afar off.

"No woman may come near a monk. But when

she did see him, she forgot all the teachings of the monks, all the prayers she came to say ; when she looked upon his face she forgot all else, as girls do.

" She was in love with the novice, and she thought always of him and of how she could tell him of her love. But it was very difficult.

" You see, she was a king's daughter, and king's daughters may only marry kings or some very high minister. There was no chance at all that she would be allowed to marry this boy, no one knew whom. There was no chance that she should ever see him near or speak to him except by some deceit.

" She lived in the palace, and no man dare come near her rooms. To any man who came near her without permission from the queen only one thing could happen, and that was death.

" When the princess went abroad she had many attendants, she went in full day, it would be quite impossible for her to appoint a meeting with the boy in some quiet place. It seemed as impossible for the princess and the boy to meet as for the stars to touch the sea.

" The queen was very wise. The palace was full of people. Even the spirits in the great thrones told her of the secrets that they heard.

The queen would know, must know, of all the princess did.

"The princess knew all this, knew it better, Thakin, than I who tell you, and yet she did not despair. She was sure she would succeed. She thought and thought and at last she hit upon a plan. This is what she did.

"Amongst her attendants there was an old woman, one who had been her nurse when she was little, who cared for her now more than any of the other attendants did, who would do for her that which no one else would do.

"And the princess called the old nurse one day quietly and told her all about it. She told her of the boy in the monastery, and how she had fallen in love with him, and without him she could not live. Something must be done ; she said she must go to the boy or the boy must come to her. Some scheme must be made, for without him she would not live. The nurse would think of some plan.

"But the nurse was horrified when she heard. That a princess, the daughter of a king, the sister of a king, should fall in love with quite a common boy in a monastery was dreadful to her. She said that she would do nothing, have no part in this business at all. The princess must forget; nothing but trouble would come of this. The princess must go no more to that monastery but must try and forget. And when the princess said she could never forget, the old nurse laughed.

"'When you are young, you say that, you think that,' she said; 'we are all that way, but when you are older it is not to forget that is hard, but to remember.'

"But the princess would not hear. Then the nurse told her how impossible it was—all dreams, nothing but dreams.

"Whatever the princess did the queen would know and then there would be trouble. There would be trouble for the princess, but for the boy worse than trouble, death. Would the princess bring her lover to death? But the princess would not hear.

"'If you plan properly,' she said, 'it will never be found out. You have only to think, and I will think too, and we will find a means.'

"For the princess was quite determined she must succeed. Not all the guards and orders of the king, not all the power and knowledge of the queen, not all the thousand prying eyes of the palace, nothing in heaven or earth, even the fear of death, should keep them apart.

"But the nurse was determined too. She

would not go to the boy, she would not help in this disaster, and she prayed the princess with tears to forget—to be wise and forget.

"It was no good. Day by day the princess grew worse. Her eyes were bright, her heart was hot, and at last one day when all her coaxing of the nurse had been no use she rose up.

" 'Very well,' she said, 'if it cannot be it cannot. But also I cannot live. The garden is near and there are tanks there where the water is cool. I will go there.'

"She ran out of her rooms and down the steps towards the gardens and the winding water-ways that lay there so cool beneath the trees. She ran with her face hot and her hair falling behind her, running very fast, caring not who saw her, and the nurse ran after her. Other people ran after her too, and just as she came near the water they came up to her and she was stopped.

" 'Will you promise?' she said, turning to the nurse as they stood there beside the dark water. 'Will you promise?'

"The nurse promised. She was afraid when she saw the princess mad like this, going to drown herself, careless of everything.

"They went back to the palace, to the princess's rooms, where every one was wondering what had come to the princess that she should run thus wildly into the garden; and there the princess gave the nurse messages to the boy, many messages, such messages as girls send, and the nurse listened, but there was in her heart quite a different message to the one the princess sent.

"The nurse went to the monastery that evening and in some way she managed to see the boy. She told him that the princess had fallen in love with him. She thought that the boy would understand all that this meant and be afraid. But he was not afraid at all; he just laughed. And then the nurse, getting angry, went on to say that this was a very terrible thing and could only end in one way. No one could be loved by a princess and live. It must be known, and the end for him would be death. There could be no other end if the matter went on. There was only one escape and that was by flight. He must run away, where the princess would never see him or hear of him again. That was the only way. But the boy would not agree. He only laughed. 'Why should I run away?' he said. 'What have I done. If the princess has fallen in love with me, is it my fault? It is pleasant to be loved by a princess. I will not run away.'

"So the boy said, Thakin, so he said. If only he had known what was to happen surely he would have been wise and gone away. But he was brave and proud. He thought it good to be loved by a girl, better still that she was a princess. He was very happy at the news and rejoiced; his eyes were bright and cheerful and he laughed with delight.

"Then the nurse got angry. The boy must run away. 'If you do not go,' she said, 'I will make you. I will go at once and tell a minister about you, and then they will send you to Mogaung at least. Probably you will be executed.'

"She was very angry that this boy would stay and trouble the heart of the princess. She hoped to frighten him and make him run away, and then the princess, not seeing him, would forget, and all would come right; but instead of being afraid he was mad with pleasure. He refused to go. He laughed at her threats. Perhaps he too loved the princess, who shall say? But he was as foolish as she was.

" 'If you,' he said to the nurse, 'go and tell any minister about it and I am arrested, I will tell all about the reason. I will say that you came to me with messages from the princess. Everybody shall know. Go and tell your minister. You know what will happen. If you are not punished by the king for acting as go-between for the princess and me the princess will have you killed for getting me into trouble; and the princess will herself come to grief. Now go and tell. But I do not know why you should wish to make us both unhappy.'

"The nurse saw that she had made a great mistake. She had never imagined that the boy would be proud and brave like this. She thought to frighten him into doing anything she wanted. Her way would have been to have gone straight to a minister and got the boy sent off without his knowing why he was sent. Then the princess' secret would have been kept. Now she saw that matters were very much worse than they were before; that instead of mending she had made them infinitely more dangerous. Before there was only a girl to deal with, now there was a boy also, both mad.

"She went back to the palace very much dispirited, and when the princess came to her and demanded whether she had seen the boy and what he had said in reply to her message, she had nothing to say. At last the nurse said that she had not been able to see the boy, that he had been with his teacher and the other monks, and that another attempt must be made. So she hid her doings from the princess.

"But the princess was very angry. 'You were

not true," she said; 'you are not telling me true. You are playing with me because you do not want me to see him. You are trying to put me off.' And she began to cry as if her heart would break. And then the nurse was sorry. She saw it was all no good her attempt to stop the princess. If the princess were denied she would do something dreadful: go to the boy herself, or drown herself in the moat. Therefore because the nurse was very fond of the princess and because she too knew what this thing that they call love is, she gave up fighting against fate and said she would help all she could.

"'Give me a letter,' she said, 'a little letter that I can hide easily, and I will take it to him. Write it to-night, and to-morrow I will go to the monastery, and if I can I will give it to him,' speaking out of the great sympathy in her heart for the girl.

"The princess went away and wrote a letter, a love letter. She wrote it very small upon a little piece of paper, which she rolled up like one of those rolls that women wear in their ears to keep the hole open and in proper shape when they do not wear their gold earrings. She wrote it very secretly so that no one should know, and next day she came and put it in the old woman's ear and sent her to the monastery.

"The woman went. She gave up trying to fight against the love of the princess and surrendered herself to fate. She went and gave the letter to the boy, slipping it into his hand by stealth as she passed him on the monastery stairs. She could not get any answer that night of course, but the princess did not mind. When she heard that her letter had reached the boy she was happy again; she clapped her hands with joy and laughed."

CHAPTER XV

LOVE AND DEATH

" Do you know what it was she wrote, Thakin ? "

" How can I know ? " I answered. " Young ladies do not write me love letters. What do they write ? Tell me."

My maid of honour laughed. She often laughs. " How do they write ? If the Thakin does not know, should I know ? "

" We are both very ignorant," I said. " We do not know much. Sometime, perhaps, we shall find out from others. But this love letter that the princess sent the boy, what was that ? "

" Ah, that was not a letter at all. It was a little love song. All women know it, and it has music to it too."

Then she began to sing to herself in curious monotones a song of which this is a translation. There are very many such love songs in Burmese, songs of men to girls, of girls to men. But they do not translate well. Of all songs love songs are the hardest to translate, their beauty depends so much upon terms of expression, on the rhythm of the lines, the music of the words.

" 'My lover is gold, he is pure gold from the furnace, and there is no speck on him. I have loved him for all my life, my days before I knew him were as naught, as forgetfulness. I have loved him all my life, I will love him for ever and for ever. Do not doubt me, my lover, never let doubt come into your thoughts, for I am not as other girls are, loving here and there, but am true far beyond death.

" ' Among the trees on the hill-top is the pagoda, you can see it from far away, all the boatmen know it. Thither will we go and pray. Together we will go, and we will pray that we may never part, not in this life nor in the next, nor the next. For a hundred lives, for a thousand eternities, we will live and love and be together.

" 'My love is pure gold. I would wear him as a necklet about my neck, that should never leave me. He is my king, my lord, and there is none in my heart but him.' "

" That was her love song, that she sent to the

boy, that many a girl has sent to many a boy ; and the woman gave it him. Next day the princess went in the morning with her attendant to the monastery to make an offering, and she saw him, the boy, her lover. Of course they could not speak, and they could only look a very little for fear people should notice, but as they came away the boy managed to pass a note to the old woman, who hid it. She could not give it to the princess then for fear of discovery, for there were many people about, but kept it. When they came to the palace the princess called her into an inner room and told her to give the letter quickly, quickly. The woman gave and the princess read her first letter from her lover. I do not know what was in it. I saw the one the princess wrote because it was found afterwards, but the one he wrote her was never found.

" After this they wrote often to each other, using always the old woman's ears ; for they were very careful, very much afraid of being found out too soon. I do not know how long this went on, but for several months. And, indeed, it seemed as if this must be the end. How could these ever be more than this, how could they ever meet—she who was a king's daughter, and he but a lad in a monastery ? After the fasting was over he left the monastery and returned to his home in Mandalay city, but this made no difference. The princess was mad. Nothing would stop her. 'We must meet!' she cried to the old nurse. 'We must meet, you must contrive a way!' And when the nurse said, 'You have his letters, cannot you be content?' the princess laughed.

"'Letters! what are letters? I want him. I want to see his face, and hear his voice, and put my hands in his. Letters, what are letters?'

"The old nurse said no more. What was the use? She would do as the princess wanted, and if trouble was to come, let it come. So the princess and nurse made a scheme between them, they planned everything, and only waited till due time to carry it out. They had to wait some time, many months, for it was necessary that the boy's hair should be grown long again. It was shaved off when he became a monk, and hair takes time to grow.

"The princess was very impatient, but there was no help for it ; even great longing will not make hair grow any faster, and after several months the nurse, who saw the boy from time to time, told her that it would do.

"Then one afternoon the nurse went out into the town. She had a bundle with her and a letter.

She went down to the house of a relation far away from the palace near the river, and there by appointment she met the boy. The nurse gave him the princess' letter and opened the bundle.

"The letter did not say much, only that the boy must do as the nurse told him and all would be well. The bundle contained clothes. 'Here,' said the nurse unfolding them, 'is one of the princess' own dresses. You must put it on quick. You must tie up your hair like a girl, and here is some false hair to add to it.' Nothing had been forgotten.

"So the boy dressed quickly, putting off his man's clothes and putting on the pink and silver skirt and white jacket of a girl. The nurse put flowers in his hair and a pearl necklace about his neck and gold bangles on his arms. Even there was cosmetic ready prepared for him to put upon his face to make it look fair, as girls do.

"He made such a pretty girl, Thakin. I saw him afterwards, ah! afterwards in the trouble. He was sad then, but by nature he had bright merry eyes, with a laugh always behind them, and full round cheeks. His hands were big for a girl to be sure, but then they took care to give him big-sleeved jackets to make his hands look smaller, and many large gold bangles to come low down and draw away the eye.

"Oh, he was very cleverly dressed. If it was the princess or the nurse who thought of it all I do not know, but it was very well done. No one would have guessed.

"So they went out, the nurse and the boy-girl, and took a trotting bullock carriage and were driven to the palace gates, and there in the half dark of evening they dismounted and passed through the western gate, the women's gate into the palace.

" The boy was passed in as the nurse's niece. She had got a pass from one of the Atwinwuns to bring in her niece, a young girl from the country, to help to attend upon the princess, and so the guards only glanced at her when they saw the pass and let her in.

"They went on through the gardens to the rooms where the princess lived. And so they met at last, those two, and loved and kissed and slept in each other's arms with the fear of death covering them like a cloak. But they did not care. They were so happy, and they did not think. What did it matter ?"

To make the end plain I must explain here what those who do not know the Burmese tongue would not understand. There are in Burmese two sets of pronouns. One is masculine and one feminine. Thus a man for "I" would say "chundaw" but a woman would say "chumma" and so on. It must have been very bewildering for one brought up as a man to say "chundaw" having to remember always to say "chumma." It is but a trifle perhaps, but it was the plan wherein the princess's little intrigue failed and it brought ruin to them both.

"They lived," went on my maid of honour, "together for months. Of course some of the attendants on the princess soon got to know that the new girl the princess loved so much was not a girl at all, but a boy. But the secret was well kept. You see, Thakin, that it was such a deadly secret that no one dared to speak of it. Had it been a little thing no doubt it would have soon been spread over the palace; but this was far too serious.

"And again it did not in any way threaten the queen or king. No doubt some of the queen's spies soon heard of it and could have told the queen of it. But they did not. Why should they hurt the princess? It could do no harm to the queen that the girl should have her lover with her. It was her own business. I suppose the secret must have come out sometime, such secrets cannot be kept for ever. There must come an end sometime. But it might have gone on for a long time yet if it had not been for an accident. Such an accident who would have suspected the way of it?

"The boy was kept very quietly in the princess's rooms, and there he was nearly safe. The old nurse was on the watch and no one could come in and discover him. But he got tired of being always shut up, even if it were with a princess as companion, and after a time when he got accustomed to things he would go out. His dress was so good, and he was so like a girl with his soft round face and fair skin that no one would guess. He had learnt too in the princess's rooms to walk like a girl and take short steps, not long strides as a man does.

"So he would go out now and again and wander about the palace gardens, sometimes with the princess as her attendant, sometimes with the nurse, sometimes alone. In this way the end came.

"It was one morning that it happened. We had got to our wait at noon, and as I came with the other maids to the room where the queen was, near the western throne, I saw that there was some great trouble. The queen looked very angry. She had a way of ruffling up her skirts to show her little bare feet when she was angry, and she had ruffled them up a great deal that day. The king was seated by her looking very troubled and all the maids were frightened to death.

"In front of the king and queen, kneeling on the floor, were two guards of the gate, the western gate; they had drawn swords in their hands, and between them knelt a girl.

"The guards were explaining to the king and the queen, and the ministers who were beside them, how the girl had come that morning near the gate. They thought she wanted to go out and so they challenged. 'Who are you?' they said, for they did not know her face. The girl looked up and answered, 'Chundaw la?' 'Are you speaking to me?' using the fatal masculine. Then the suspicions of the guard were aroused.

"'Who are you?' they said; 'what sort of girl can you be who answer like a man?'

"They arrested this would-be girl, and soon enough discovered all about everything. There was the lad kneeling before the king, grey with fear, for he knew his time was come. He could not speak for very horror, and he panted for breath with quick short pants. We were all so sorry for him, he was such a pretty boy, and all the prettier in his girl's dress.

"Presently through the door and up the steps

came the princess. She had been sent for by the
king. I do not think she knew at first why she
had been sent for, because she looked about in
surprise wondering why every one looked so very
serious. But when she saw her lover there she
understood. It all came to her in a flash that the
end was come, the certain end. She became very
pale and for a moment she seemed as if she would
die there at once. But quickly she recovered, she
was such a brave girl, and she moved forward,
and knelt before the king, kneeling so that she
could see her lover. She did not care for any one
else, only for him, she did not look at any one else,
only at him. She tried to catch his look that she
might smile to him. But he never looked at her.
He looked only at the guard. I do not think he
knew she was there. He was quite distraught,
and his fingers moved to and fro on the floor.
The princess's eyes became full of tears when she
saw him so.

"There was an inquiry. It did not take long,
for the princess confessed at once. It was all her
fault she said, the boy was not to blame. If
any one was to be punished it must be she, for it
was by her orders that the boy had been brought
into the palace. She pleaded and pleaded for the
boy.

"The king looked sorry but the queen grew more and more angry. She was especially furious at the love letter, the little love song which the princess had written to her lover. It was found on him with other letters of hers, when he was searched at the gate. He had always carried them with him. The queen said it was disgraceful that any one should behave so, much more a princess. She, the queen, was always trying to tell the people to act properly, and here in the palace a princess behaved as if she did not know what modesty was.

"Ah, Thakin, it was such a scene, a terrible end to all their love-making. I can see it now, as if it was before me. The room with gold and red pillars, and the sad king, and the angry queen, and the princess and——"

My maid of honour's voice began to quaver, and she stopped here and began to cry softly, she was so sorry for them both. Her tender heart went out to their trouble. What a scene it was for a child to have witnessed.

"Thakin," she said, "I am so sorry. I did not intend to cry. But telling you of it all seemed to make it come so near to me again. Telling you of them seemed to bring their faces back to me as if it was not all long ago. They come to me out of the night as a dream. But I will tell you the end now. There is not much more.

"The inquiry was soon over for there was no doubt. No one denied what had happened. The boy, still in his girl's dress, was led away, and the princess followed.

"They were condemned, indeed there was no chance for them. For though the king would have pardoned them the queen would not have it. She was very angry. She might perhaps have overlooked the fault of the princess but for one thing. When they came to search in the boy's house in the town they found a great number of letters that the princess had written to him before he came to live in the palace, and these letters said things about the queen that she could not bear. They were all brought to her, and she read them, and when she read them she became furious. All pity went away out of her heart, and she became mad. First of all she wished to make the princess into a pagoda slave. She wanted to make her into one of those who have to attend at the pagodas, and who are outcasts from all the people, and she consulted the ministers about it. But they said it could not be done.

"'The princess,' they said, 'is the queen's sister. If then, the princess be made a pagoda slave, the queen's family will be dishonoured. She will be sister to a slave. Can the queen allow that? The foreigners would all say, " See now the queen of Burma, she is of a family of pagoda slaves! " It cannot be.'

" The queen agreed that it could not be, but that the princess was to be killed.

"One day they were led out, the princess and the boy, to the cemetery without the gates to be killed. They were put into carts and taken through the city, and many people followed, and when they came to the cemetery they were told to get out. So they got out and stood and looked at each other, the girl hard and proud still, and full of love for the boy, but he was half dead with fear. And when the princess saw him thus with lack lustre eyes waiting the death that was to come she called out to her attendants to give her the golden bowl of water. They gave it to her and she went to the boy and held it to him. ' Take it,' she said, ' my last gift.' The boy took it and drank, and they prepared for death.

" But death did not come. For some reason the queen changed her mind and sent to the cemetery and stopped the execution, and they were led back. But the hope was not for long. The boy was soon taken away to one of the islands and tied up in a

THE END OF THE PRINCESS' LOVER

sack with large stones, and thrown by night into the waters of the great river. No one can love a princess and live.

"And the girl? She was confined in a special prison, and before long she too was dead. They said she caught a cold and died, but how should I know? Death is very sudden sometimes when you are a prisoner."

CHAPTER XVI

THE LOTTERIES

"What were all the lotteries that people talk about so much?" I asked. "There were many lotteries, they say, and many people were ruined, and many committed suicide, is that so?" My maid of honour laughed.

"Ah! Thakin, those lotteries. Such a thing they were. They were got up by one of the ministers. The revenue was falling short. Money did not come in as it used to do, and much money was spent by the queen on her jewels and other things. So one day a minister proposed a lottery to the king. It should be quite fair he said, and it was done by many foreign governments.

"You had a lottery and gave prizes, and you paid all the prizes honestly. But you kept a certain part of the money for yourself as commission.

"The people would like the lotteries, and they would many of them take tickets. And so the people would enjoy themselves greatly, and the king would get much revenue. Moreover the revenue would be paid as it were willingly, and the people would not grumble.

"The king agreed and the lotteries were got up.

"There were two kinds of lottery, the little lottery and the big one. The little lottery was this. There were sixty balls put into a box, and one of them was a gold ball. That was the one that won. You could stake on any number up to sixty. The way you staked was by buying tickets. In the great lottery-house in the city were many little stalls kept mostly by women ; you went to one and said, 'I wish to stake one rupee upon the number thirty-six.' Then she gave you a ticket saying you had staked the money on the number and you went away. If you wanted to stake a large sum you had probably to go to several stall holders and stake with each, for one stall holder could not take a large sum. They were poor people who paid for their stalls to the minister who held the lottery.

"At noon each day the lottery was drawn. A great gong sounded, and the people came running to the lottery-house to see the lottery. A minister was in attendance and a guard. There was a sort of drum with the balls in it. The drum had a spout, and the balls came out one at a time.

"The gong was struck, and the drum was rolled round, and a man stood up and called out 'Number one.' Then a ball was allowed to run out. Number two was called out, and another ball was allowed to run out, and so on. To whatever number the golden ball came the prize was awarded.

"Directly the golden ball came out the crowd broke up and the winners ran away to the stall holders to get their money. They were paid forty-eight times their stake. Thus if you staked one anna you got three rupees. If you staked ten rupees you got four hundred and eighty rupees.

"Sometimes however you did not get the money. Perhaps the stall holder had too much money on the winning number and could not pay. Then if any one complained the woman was arrested, and perhaps instead of getting your winnings a man would come to you and say, 'What a sad thing! The poor woman has been arrested and put in gaol. Will you not give something to get her out?' So you were sorry and gave a rupee or two in addition to your losses.

"However, generally you got paid. That was the little lottery. It was drawn every day at noon.

"The great lottery was different. There the tickets were five rupees each, and they were numbered up to three or four thousand. The first prize was ten thousand rupees and there were smaller prizes. It was only drawn once a month. You could take one ticket or as many as you liked. There was a great ceremony when it was drawn and the lucky winner was at once called up and given a title by the minister in charge. He was called 'The honourable rich man.' Every one made obeisance to him. Then he was put on a gaily caparisoned elephant, and his bags of silver were piled up by his side, and he was paraded through the streets with a guard of honour, so that all should see him. It was a grand affair and the man who won was nearly mad with delight and pride.

"It was of course a great thing to win in the big lottery, but it was not such fun as the little lottery. There you staked what you liked, as little as one anna, and the lottery was drawn every day.

"All the palace people gambled at it. Some of the princesses were nearly mad about it, and they staked every day. When their money was gone they got more from the queen, and when the queen would not give any more, they pawned their jewels and gold bracelets, everything they had. They never any of them won. And yet they took great pains to win. They would consult fortune tellers and stake on the numbers they told to them, and they would watch omens, and they would dream.

" Every night they would go to bed hoping to dream of the lucky number, and every morning there was a great comparison of dreams and discussion of their meaning. Every one tried to dream. Still they lost.

" I think now the reason was this. They could not of course go themselves to take tickets, and perhaps the women who took tickets for them were not honest. Otherwise surely sometimes they would win. But they never won and many of them were ruined quite, and the queen was very angry with them.

" In the city it was worse. Men and women gambled and gambled until they lost all. If they lost to begin with they went on gambling hoping to get it back. If they won they thought they had found a sure way to fortune, much better than trading or working or cultivating land, and they went on till all was lost. Then many of them committed suicide.

" Such ruin as this lottery caused through the whole country you cannot imagine, Thakin. Men quarrelled with their wives and wives with their husbands. Boys went and stole to get money to gamble with and girls threw all decency to the winds and rushed to the gaming booths.

" The losers became robbers and waited at the gaming houses to note the winners and follow them home and rob them. Murders happened every day.

" It was terrible. Such tragedies as there were. One of them I remember very well. There were a man and a woman newly married. They were quite young and they were very fond of each other and they had a good trade and did well. Then the lotteries began. At first they gambled just a little, one anna or two annas just for fun, but after a little they grew fond of the excitement and they went on and staked more and more. Little by little they lost all they had.

" All their money went first and then they pawned their jewels, and these went, and then they pawned their house and their clothes and all they had. They lost and lost until one day all that was left to them of the property that had been theirs was ten rupees.

" That night the woman dreamt a dream. She thought she was at the gambling house watching the lottery. There were the ministers there and the guard of soldiers and the crowd of people. The gong was rung and the numbers were called out. She heard them called and saw the balls roll out of the drum and the disappointed looks of those who had tickets on the smaller numbers.

" The numbers went on and on and no golden ball came out for a long time, and then at last it came.

" Thirty-seven ! " shouted the clerk and the drum rattled and the ball rolled out, and lo, it was the golden ball at last. Thirty-seven had won. And amid the shouts of the crowd she awoke.

" She told her husband the dream, and they determined that now at last a true dream had come to them and they would win. Not a word did they say to any one, but it was decided that the husband should stake the last money they had, their last ten rupees, upon number thirty-seven. They would surely win, and with four hundred and eighty rupees they would be well off again. But the wife would not go herself. 'No,' she said, 'I will not go. I cannot bear it. But do you go. And if you win then shall you do this that I may know. If you win you shall come out of the north gate of the gaming house, and down this street from the north that I may see you afar off, and know that we have won. But if you lose then come out of the south gate, and up the street the south way. Then shall I know that all is over. It is our last chance.'

"The husband went to the gaming house and waited. And just as the wife had dreamt so it happened. The numbers came out one, two, three, four, no golden ball; five, six, and on and on up to thirty-six, and at thirty-seven out it rolled, the bright gold ball of hope and happiness. The man went nearly mad with delight. He shrieked and howled and beat his arms and ran to the stall holders and got the money and tore away home to tell his wife and pour the silver stream before her. He was so mad with hope and with delight that he forgot. What his wife had told him had quite fallen away out of his memory and he ran by the shortest way to his house, the way he had always gone before, the south way.

"And when he got home he found his wife hanging from the cross-beam just dead. She had seen him coming running like a madman up the south way and she had thought that he had lost and so hanged herself. The street was long and she was dead ere he arrived.

"There were many stories as bad as this.

"It spread like a fever throughout the country. Men and women came from far-away towns and villages to gamble at Mandalay till the city was full of ruined houseless wretches.

"Then at last the king and queen put an end

to the lotteries. They had brought much money into the treasury, but when the king and queen heard the tales that were told them of the ruin going on in the country, and when they looked round and saw how many in the palace had lost all, that the princesses were without jewels and the pages without money, the lotteries were stopped. It was time indeed that they were ended or the whole nation would have been ruined. Trade would have come to an end and the land would not have been cultivated and the villages would have been deserted.

"As it was, terrible harm was done.

"But even though they had lost, the palace people were sorry when the lotteries ceased. They were something to talk about, it was something to do to stake at the little lottery. It was a relief from the everlasting plotting of the palace folk to have a little gamble."

CHAPTER XVII

THE LITTLE PRINCESS

" There were no end to the plots that went on in the palace, Thakin. You do not suppose that the queen-mother had ever forgotten how her plots failed, her plots that she was to be the real ruler of Burma and the king but a puppet in her hands. She had picked out King Thibaw for that reason because he was weak, and she would be able to rule him, and now she had less power than ever because her second daughter had obtained such control over the king that no one else had a word to say. You do not suppose that she had forgotten this.

" And the ministers, were they likely to forget ? Under King Mindon they had power and authority and had each his own place, and now they were flouted and laughed at and made of no account. Do you think that they could forget, when every day they were made to feel that there was no power or authority in the land save that of the queen ?

They were humbled before the people and they were not likely to forget. And so there were plots.

"What these plots were no one can be sure, nor who took part in them, because they were kept so secret that no one could discover exactly. But the queen suspected. She was always suspecting, and she had always spies looking and listening to discover what was going on.

"Amongst us maids of honour there were a few Shan girls, and these were very useful to the queen. For they had no friends in the palace people. They were the queen's maids, and looked only to her and cared not for others.

"They had no relations to gossip with. Moreover, they were stupid and wild and ill-mannered, and could do things which none of us could do. If people were talking, one of these girls would go and sit down near and listen.

"The talkers would not mind her. 'It is only a wild Shan girl,' they said ; 'probably she does not know Burmese. Anyhow, she is too foolish to understand.'

"And again, one of these girls would suddenly walk into the queen-mother's rooms and sit down and see all that was going on and who was there. Being a Shan girl, she would be excused for her rudeness because she did not know. No one of us would have dared to do such a thing. Besides, we would have been suspected. But these girls went everywhere and heard everything, and told the queen.

"So it came to the queen's ears that there was a plot. King Thibaw was to be dethroned somehow or other, and one of the banished princes recalled and made king. Which it was I do not know.

"This new king was to be married to her sister the little princess. King Thibaw had married two sisters, the elder princess and the second princess who was now queen. The new king would marry the little princess, the youngest daughter of the queen-mother, and so she would be queen-mother still. Such was the plot.

"The head of the plot was the queen-mother. Others were concerned in it, of course, but I do not know who they were.

"The queen-mother being in the plot made matters very difficult for the queen. For she was afraid of her mother.

"It is true she had usurped all the power, but nevertheless the queen-mother was a person not to be overlooked. The queen could not imprison her or execute her as she would have done any lesser person.

"So the queen could only watch and wait. Once or twice she caught people who had carried messages to the princes in Calcutta, and these she severely punished, but that could not end the plot. It went on and on and became very serious.

"A curious accident brought matters to a climax. There was a fortune teller in the palace, and the princesses and the maids of honour were fond of getting him to come in and tell their fortunes. He always told good fortunes. He said that you would be lucky and get a good husband and have money, and so on. Only he always said that to get your fortune you must be religious and good, otherwise the fortune would not come. Thus he was very cunning, for if anything went wrong with one of his predictions he was always able to say that it was your own fault, that you had not followed his advice, you had been irreligious or wicked.

"One day it was reported to the queen that this fortune teller had been telling the fortunes of the princesses. He had told them that they would be queens.

"When the queen heard this there was such a disturbance !

"The queen nearly went out of her mind with anger, and the whole palace was turned upside down. An official was despatched in a fearful hurry to fetch him. He was not to be found in the palace, and to save time the official went rushing out of the west gate, the women's gate.

" That was an almost unheard-of thing to do, but the queen was in such a frantic state of mind that there was no time to think of this.

"The fortune teller was found in his house and rushed off to the palace at once. Of course he was to be executed.

" He was taken in, and as he went through the corridors a page met him and hit him. They were only too glad in the palace always to hit a man in disgrace. The page hit him and knocked him down, but he was pulled up and dragged before the queen. There he sat all dishevelled, and the queen glared at him.

" ' We have heard,' said the queen, ' that you have been telling the princesses that they will be queens. That is, of course, untrue. We cannot have lies like this told in the palace, so you are to be executed at once. Whose fortunes have you been telling ? '

" Then the fortune teller spoke. He was a cunning man and knew his life was at stake, and he spoke well. ' It is true,' he answered, ' that I have been telling the fortune of a princess. I told her fortune and the queen's fortune long ago, and I said they would be queens. It has been true. Now I have been telling the elder princess's fortune again. I said to her, "I foretold that you would be queen. You have been queen. Now are you queen no longer. So it will be all the rest of your life. You will never be queen again." That is the fortune I told her.'

"When the queen heard this her rage all went at once. She fancied she had been mistaken. She never paused to ask if he had been telling fortunes to any of the other princesses. The fortune teller's reply had pleased her so much that she forgot. All the rage went out of her face and she turned to the king and said, 'Truly this is what he told me long ago, that I should be queen, and it has come true. I think, too, this man is the man who told our fortunes when we first came to the palace. He is a worthy man. He should be, rewarded.'

"The king, only too glad to see the queen in a good temper again, agreed. Orders were given to reward the fortune teller. He was given a post as clerk to the chief court, and he had a lot of money given to him, and he was ordered to be held in honour.

"And so the fortune teller who was brought

188

into the palace to be executed went out half an hour later a wealthy and respected man.

" Such was life in the palace. You could not tell from one moment to another what would happen, and generally what you least expected that was what occurred.

" But this episode of the fortune teller reminded the queen about the plots, and the princess her younger sister. As to the other princesses, her half-sisters, she was not afraid of them, but her younger sister was a real danger to her and she recognised it. Something must be done. So the queen thought and thought and at last an idea came to her.

" The plot that she was afraid of was a plot of the queen-mother. She wanted to have a daughter as queen, and a king who would be easily ruled. She had put King Thibaw on the throne with the idea. She had married him to the elder princess with but this idea. But it had failed. The middle princess had come in and spoiled the whole arrangement. Two of her daughters were married, but a third still remained. All the queen-mother's hopes and plots were based on her. Without her the plots would have no meaning. If then, thought the queen, the little princess were out of the way an end must come to the plot at once.

"The queen saw this. She did not want to hurt her little sister. She would not punish her in any way, for even there in the palace you must have some justification for any punishment. She could not marry the girl to any officer because she was a princess, and could not marry a commoner. There was but one way, and that was that the girl must be married to the king. Then would King Thibaw be husband to all the queen-mother's daughters, and there would be no use in putting up a new king for there would be no one for him to marry.

"That was the queen's idea. Thus would she utterly defeat the queen-mother, and besides do an act which the people would praise rather than blame.

"So she sent for her little sister and spoke kindly to her.

"'You are a princess,' she said, 'and I would like to see you married. For it is a good thing to be married and every woman ought to have a husband. But with you it is difficult because you are a princess and can only marry royal blood. I cannot give you to a minister or an official, so I have thought about it, and because I have great affection for you, I will give you to the king for his wife. Then shall we all live together and be very happy.'

"But the little princess shook her head.

"'No, no!' she said. 'It is very kind of you, and the king would be a good husband. But you are very fond of him, and why should he take another wife? No! It would be better not.'

"Then the queen coaxed her and said, 'See now, you will be a queen. How fine that will be! Every one will honour you. To be an unmarried girl, what is the use of that?'

"But the little princess would not hear of it.

"'I do not want to be a queen. To be unmarried, how pleasant that is! There is no worry, no trouble. But to be a queen is a great trouble. You my sister are always worried about this or about that, while I live in great peace. I would rather be as I am. I am now very happy.'

"So the queen persuaded, and the little princess refused. Then at last the queen became angry and said, 'I have spoken to you nicely and been kind to you because you are my sister and I am sorry for you. You do not want to marry the king. But you *must* marry the king. It is my order, and you must.'

"The little princess was afraid with this, and at last she gave way and agreed that she would marry the king.

" As to the king there was no trouble with him. He was ready enough to marry any one or do anything that the queen told him. He agreed readily enough, and there was no one else to consult. The queen was all powerful in the palace, and if she wanted her little sister to marry the king no one could object. It was soon done. No ceremony was required. The queen gave her sister to the king as wife, and there was an end to it.

" But every one was sorry for the poor little princess. It is true that she was not banished to her own apartments as was the elder princess. She lived with the king and queen, and went about with them. But she had a hard life of it. For although the little princess was very quiet and easy going, and the queen had never any cause to fear that she might take the king from her, yet she hated her nevertheless. She could not bear to have any one with her near the king. Even her sister, the quiet inoffensive little girl, was hateful to her. She treated her very unkindly often, and seemed to rejoice in humiliating her before the palace people, so that people should clearly understand that there was but one queen. Of course the little princess had never a word to say in affairs of state. No one cared for her or consulted her. Though she was a lesser queen she might still have been an unmarried princess for all the difference it made.

" This act of the queen of course put an end to the plots. The queen-mother had now no more daughters to marry. It would be no good for her to plot against King Thibaw, and dethrone him. Her daughters were his wives. Though King Thibaw be killed, yet could his wives never marry again. Such was the etiquette of the court. All the queen-mother's interest was now bound up in the king. The queen was far too clever for her, was far too clever and too determined for any one."

CHAPTER XVIII

THE CLOUD IN THE SOUTH

THUS amidst plots and intrigues, dangers and games, passed away six years. While the queen had been fighting her fight in the palace and was winning her victory, making herself the sole ruler of the kingdom, this kingdom had been slipping slowly from her hands. While the king and queen frolicked in their gardens and played within the palace, the government that King Mindon their father had built up crumbled away and enemies came and watched. There had been warnings before. The British envoy had made remonstrance upon remonstrance, without effect.

Perhaps the fault here was not all on the side of the Burmese government. The envoy seems to have been without tact sometimes. The ministers were fiercely resentful of his attitude and of what they declared to be his misrepresentation of facts. Very soon the situation became impossible, and in

October 1879, he was withdrawn amid expressions of delight and relief from the court and the people.

The hated envoy was gone and now there would be peace. Yet was there no peace.

Though the Indian government had now no envoy at the Burmese court, yet it was still able to write letters, to remonstrate, to threaten, and it did all these things. Good grounds for grievance were not lacking on one side or the other.

Then the Burmese, fearing what might happen, tried to make themselves friends elsewhere. They sent embassies to other European countries to try and make friends there; they welcomed from them envoys to their own court. Steadily, if slowly, matters grew worse, wanting but for a spark to cause an explosion.

Then a curious belief had grown up amongst the mercantile community of India and Burma, that Upper Burma was a very wealthy country. It was a land they imagined full of gold and silver, of coal and petroleum, of jade and of amber, containing the richest ruby mines in the world. Wheat grew there and cotton; it was immensely fertile, capable of producing all sorts of staples in enormous quantities.

The reason why all these remained undeveloped, they imagined, was simply the bad government

of the king. Remove that and no one could esti-
mate what would happen in the way of increased
trade. The people, they thought, groaned under a
brutal tyranny, a hideous system of monopolies
that bound them down to poverty amidst immense
potential wealth.

It was imagined, too, that the Burmese themselves acknowledged this, that they were restive
under a yoke that was upon them, and would be
delighted to free themselves from it. Any one
would be welcomed who would assist the people to
recover their liberty which they had lost.

Now, when we know that most of Upper Burma
is really a very poor country, with a decreasing
rainfall, many parts of it chronically verging on
famine, this view of the wealth of Upper Burma
seems ludicrous.

We know now, too, that, while not exactly
admiring the rule of King Thibaw and his
ministers, the Burmese people preferred him to
being reduced to subjection under a foreign
dominion.

How any other view could have been held is the
cause for astonishment. But perhaps the truth
may be that these views were not actually, soberly
considered and accepted, but rather wished for and
desired and so assumed to be true.

However that may be, the troubles between the two Powers, that had resulted in the wars of 1825 and 1852, that had been allowed to slumber on both sides during the reign of King Mindon, broke out again as soon as King Mindon died.

Of the justice of the quarrel this is not the place to consider; no doubt there were good grounds for complaints on both sides. The Burmese were angry at what they stated was the misrepresentation of the envoy and of the misunderstanding of their acts by the Indian government. The Indian government, on its side, was annoyed at the treatment of the envoy, at the missions to foreign courts, at disturbances on the frontier, which were not, it said, suppressed as they should be.

When two governments march for several hundred miles of frontier and are not on good terms there are plenty of things to quarrel about. But the great disagreement was not on any of these things. Whatever may have been the secret causes at work, the ostensible reason for the war was simple enough.

There are in Upper Burma vast teak forests. The timber out of these forests is the finest teak in the world. You can get teak elsewhere—from Siam and the Andamans and a little from India—but it is not equal in quality to the Burmese wood. For shipbuilding and any work that requires great strength and durability there is no wood like Burmese teak.

The forests, therefore, are of great value, and the principal ones were leased by the Burmese government to an English firm called the Bombay-Burma Trading Corporation, Limited, which has its headquarters in Bombay. They established agencies here and there, and had the teak girdled and felled and dragged by elephants into the creeks. Thence the floods carried the logs into the rivers, where it was rafted for Rangoon. The leases were granted under certain restrictions as to the size of the timber exported and the duty payable thereon.

Sometime in 1884, I think, the Burmese government stated that they had discovered that these conditions had been infringed. Large sized timber had, through the collusion of corrupt Burmese officials, been passed through the government frontier station as undersized timber, and a great fraud had been committed causing a very heavy loss to the revenue. A stringent inquiry was instituted and it was proved—so the Burmese government said—that this had been going on for a long time.

The Corporation of course denied the whole matter, but the Burmese government were convinced, and they ordered the Corporation to pay the revenue which they estimated they had been defrauded of, and a further heavy sum as fine, amounting in all to about a quarter of a million sterling. There was talk too of cancelling the leases.

The Corporation were wealthy, but a fine of such magnitude, especially if in addition the leases had been cancelled, meant something very like ruin, and they appealed to the Indian government.

Anxious to protect a wealthy firm like this from the calamity that menaced them the Indian government made overtures to the Burmese government. What the course of all these negotiations was I do not know, but they all failed. As the previous attempt of the Corporation to win to their side the queen and the most powerful ministers had failed, so the interference of the Indian government in their favour failed also.

The Burmese government were firm. " This Corporation," they said, "are swindlers. They have been fairly tried and there is no doubt of it. They have defrauded the government of a vast amount of revenue and corrupted our officials to try and hide their evil doings. The king of Burma is king and will do what he thinks just and right even should the evil doers be Englishmen. Sentence has been passed and cannot be revoked. The fine must be paid or all the leases will be at once cancelled."

In words such as these the Burmese government replied to the negotiations of the Indian government.

There was, however, no great haste to enforce this decree. The Burmese government was in no very great hurry, and matters drifted on through the hot weather of 1885, the cloud growing more and more black, the certainty of war nearer and nearer. The country began to be full of rumours. Men were eneasy, expecting they knew not quite what, sure that trouble was about to betide them. It was said that the Burmese government sent emissaries to the lower country to stir up sedition. An artillery colonel went up to Mandalay to examine the defences of the city and make plans of it so that our generals would know what they were about. He was detected but escaped in time, the captain of the trading steamer who brought him up very nearly paying for this assistance to a spy with his life. The Burmese government were angered at this mission of the colonel to spy out their deficiences and wrote indignantly about it to Rangoon, where their remonstrance was treated as an impertinence.

So matters grew from bad to worse.

Meanwhile troops were being sent over to Burma from India and all preparations were being made for an advance on Mandalay as soon as the worst of the rains were over. Mandalay lies on the Irrawaddy, about 700 miles by river above Rangoon and 400 miles above our frontier station of Thayetmyo, and it was by river that the expedition was to move. Many river steamers were chartered and armed with big guns and flats were fitted to carry the troops. The preparations were rapid and thorough.

On the king's part, too, some preparation was made, not very much. Some troops were sent down from Mandalay to Minhla and to the frontier on the east, and efforts were made to raise and arm more men. But there was no discipline, no order. There was no Bundoola in these latter days to lead armies for the king. It is incredible what ignorance, what want of knowledge and method and even common honesty there was. Money was given to be paid to the troops, but it never reached them; arms were paid for but not received. Nowhere was there any guiding hand, any wise head to see the way and follow it. It is true that the Kinwun Mingyi's advice was always for peace and for smoothing down things and doing the best he could. But then he was but one, and what was wanted was not advice but knowledge.

If the king and queen had only understood! But they did not. They knew nothing of the world outside of their palace. They thought they were in power and wisdom equal to any kings in the world and strong enough to speak with any enemy in the gate. Therefore, when the Kinwun Mingyi advised submission they naturally put down his advice to cowardice or to even worse, to treachery.

Why should they submit? They were sure they were right in what they were doing. The interference of the Indian government between the Burmese government and the Corporation appeared to the king and his councillors to be out of place. They were sure England dared not do so with, say, France or America or Russia; why then with them?

That the difference lay in the fact that these nations are strong and mighty and well able to resent interference, whereas Burma was so weak as to be a prey to any one who chose, never occurred to them.

No one told them the truth; no one dared, on the penalty of being convicted of previous falsehood. Knowledge remained without the palace gates—knowledge and fear. Inside were ignorance and courage. They lived, these children, in a dream, a beautiful dream of glory and strength and majesty. No one dared to hint to them that they stood no sort of chance in a quarrel with England. The Kinwun Mingyi offered advice, he dared not tell the truth. Hints of his were misunderstood, or disregarded.

The king and his government acted all through as if they had behind them an invincible army. All their messages of those days to the British government are instinct with a sense of dignity and strength, absolute confidence in their own rectitude of action, in their own power to repulse any attempt at interference.

To me now, looking back, it seems full of the deepest pathos, this situation of these young people. Their childish ignorance, their terrible weakness, their dignified assumption of power and strength. Surely nothing could be more pitiable than this, knowing as we do whither it led them.

Such was the situation at the end of the rains in 1885.

CHAPTER XIX

THE LAST FESTIVAL OF THE FULL MOON

"It was the custom," said my maid of honour, "at the great feast on the full moon of October, the end of our months of fasting, that all the ministers and soldiers and officials of all kinds should come and pay their respects to the king.

"A reception was held in the eastern throne room, beneath the great spire of the 'centre of the universe.' The huge doors were thrown wide open and guards stood on the steps in rows with bright swords and guns in their hands and embossed spears, between whom the visitors walked into the throne room.

"And there in the throne room amid the blaze of gold and colour on the walls and pillars, sat the king with his great ministers.

"He did not sit upon the throne. King Thibaw never dared to sit on the throne of King Mindon. For King Mindon his father was a great king, wise and firm and strong, knowing the hearts of his people and the ways of the world. He was worthy of a great throne. King Thibaw knew himself to be no man like his father. He knew that he was young and weak and very ignorant, not at all worthy to sit on the throne his father had sat upon.

"So the great golden gates behind the throne were never opened, the great golden seat was never occupied. King Thibaw sat down below at the foot of the throne on a cushion. He leaned one arm upon the base of the throne as if he would say, 'If I do not yet ascend the throne because I am young and not very clever, yet it is mine. This throne is mine, and some day when I am grown older and wiser I too shall sit upon it.'

"Perhaps that was in his mind, but the time never came, never will come in which any shall sit upon that golden throne, hold audience from there of all his people.

"The king sat below the throne on a cushion, with the ministers beside him, and great numbers of people came to his audience.

"Every man who ate of the bread of the king in Mandalay must come, ministers and judges and secretaries, soldiers and engineers and the officers of the king's boats. Even many officials came from distant provinces to pay honour to the king on that day.

"Every minister wore his robe of office. Each kind of high official had his own proper robe, and they must wear them in Mandalay so that you could tell who each man was, and pay him due respect if you met him. But on the reception day they wore special robes and the tall headdress which makes the face look wise and solemn.

"While the king held his reception in the eastern throne room, the queen held hers in her own throne room, the western room. She, too, sat at the foot of the throne leaning her arm upon it as the king did. Thakin, she was a greater queen than any queen of King Mindon's, but still she would not ascend the throne. As the king did not she could not. And she, too, was very young.

"At this their last reception the king was but twenty-seven and the queen twenty-six years old.

"While the ministers and soldiers went to the king, their wives and daughters came to the queen. Such a crowd there was coming through the great doors and up the steps to the throne room. As we sat by the queen we saw them come up the steps from the gardens to the terrace, and then from the terrace up the stairs between the great golden pillars. Very gay they were with their

206

bright beautiful silks and thin white jackets, wearing many gold bracelets and all sorts of jewels.

"There were few old people among them. The queen was young, and the young come to the court of the young. Very many of them were pretty, too, and all so pleased to be received by the queen.

"She sat there by the throne with princesses and maids of honour about her, a glory of gold and jewels, and as the new comers were introduced to her one by one, she said a word to them, a pleasant word always. There was nothing the queen liked more than these receptions. There were only two a year, so she did not get tired of them, and with all these people coming to bow to her she felt she was queen indeed.

"That was the last reception the queen ever held, the last time that many of her people saw her face. I shall never see a sight like that again, so gay, so beautiful, so glad.

"Then we had boat races upon the moat outside the city walls.

"It is a capital place for boat races, as it is long and straight and there is no current, and as only two boats race at one time there is plenty of breadth.

"The king and queen did not go. Every one

wanted them to go but they would not. They were so fond of the palace, they did not care to move out of it. But we had leave to go, and many of us went. We were driven down through the city to the outer side where the races were being held, and there was a nice covered place made all ready for us, and we sat there and watched.

"There were a great number of boats from all parts: from Sagaing and Ava and many other places on the river. They were very pretty with gilding, and the paddles were gilded on the blades so that they flashed through the water like sunlight. Before the race each boat came out and rowed about a little and a man danced and sang in the bows and the paddlers answered in chorus.

"With the boats came a great number of villagers, friends, and relations of the paddlers, and they ran on the bank and shouted with the excitement. Then there were people betting great sums of money. Each village would lay on its own boat every penny they had, and the men went to pawn their silk head-cloths to get another rupee to put on. The ministers, too, were betting, and the pages were like mad boys laying money here and there on whatever boat they thought had the best style as the crew paddled. The maids of honour also betted. When they had no money they betted their bracelets and their jewels. I, too, betted and won twenty rupees."

I looked scandalised, and she laughed.

"Ah, the Thakin is much shocked. English ladies never bet; and the Thakin when he plays cards——"

"You were telling me about the boat-race," I interrupted. "Cards are quite a different subject from boat-races. How many paddlers were there in each boat?"

"Some had sixty, some not so many, but I do not think any had so few as thirty, all young men, so handsome and so strong. They started away down the moat and raced towards us. There was a dead silence as they were preparing for the start. When the boats were off there was a murmur and then silence again, men holding their breath with excitement. The boats came rushing through the water towards us, the white foam flying from their sides and the paddles flashing so quickly to-and-fro. Now one gained, now another, as they quickened and slackened. Men were so excited they fell into the moat, and no one even laughed. At the end came the last rush, the crews shouting in time and the bow paddlers standing up to seize upon the cane strung through the bamboo, the badge of victory. Then came a tremendous roar, every one shouting at once. All the dense mile of people on both sides of the water swayed and surged and shouted as if they were madmen. Men who had won leaped and threw their arms in the air and laughed out aloud. The friends of the winning boat were mad with joy, and the friends of the losing boat shook their heads and said: 'Never mind; next time we shall beat you into pieces. Our men were a little tired to-day.'

" Then everything quieted down for the next race.

" Nearly all day the races went on, and in the evening the queen sent presents for the winning boats. She sent them down by a maid of honour, the daughter of a high official. The winning crews were called up and the presents were given to them in the name of the queen. And while the people were shouting with joy and the sunlight fell in level rays upon the shining water and the nodding lotus leaves, upon the great red walls of the city and the ever-moving people, we drove away back to the palace.

" Such a day of pleasure for the people, Thakin. There are never any boat-races on the moat now for the people to enjoy. They work hard and there are no pleasures made for them. No one cares for them now.

"At night the palace gardens were lit up. Lamps were hung upon the trees, and there were little clusters of lights behind the bamboo clumps and flower bushes. All the bridges that crossed the waterways were lined with lamps, and the summer-house was as if it were built with fire. All the gardens both on the north and south twinkled with myriads of lights, and the still waters of the canals gave them back again twice over.

"In front of the western throne room we had a maze. It was built of bamboo trellis-work about two feet high at the outside, rising gradually to the centre. In the centre was a trophy of painted panels and gilding very beautiful, and at each corner of the maze was another smaller trophy.

All along the trellis there were little lamps, so that as you stood on the palace steps you saw the whole maze in gold and crimson flame. It was great fun trying to get into the maze, but very difficult. You must not jump over any of the partitions, but find your way properly to the centre. Many of us tried, but few of us got in, and when we wandered along and came to a full stop and had to come back, those outside who were watching laughed.

"Neither the king nor queen tried the maze, but stood and watched and laughed, and wandered now and then through the gardens to see the lights on the bridges and behind the trees. There was music too playing, and a dance going on in the portico, and all sorts of amusements. Overhead was the full moon, so that even when the lamps waned and died the world was full of light. Only the shadows were more dense. All that night no one thought of sleep. For there were the gardens to roam in and the pwès to watch, and then there was the great weaving going on.

"For it is custom to give many presents to the monks at the end of Lent, especially new robes, and there was always a keen competition about these robes.

"The great ladies of the palace, the princesses and the wives of the ministers and officials, made up parties to weave these robes. They were woven in the palace during the night of the ' full moon. Spinning wheels were brought in, and looms and dyeing vats and cotton. Nothing else was allowed. No ready-woven cloth nor any thread, just only the carded cotton. At a given time the ladies began to work. The cotton had to be spun into

thread and sized and dyed and woven all in a night.
Such a tremendous hurry there was! Girl suc
ceeded girl. As soon as one was tired another
began, and worked as hard as she could for a
little time, and she then gave way to another.
The desire of each party was to have their robe
finished in time to present to the monks next
morning. All night long there was feverish hurry
at the work, all the ladies laughing and working
and taking a little doze and working again.

"Then the queen would go round and see how the
work progressed, and encourage the workers, and
perhaps lend a maid of honour here and another
there to parties that were behindhand.

"There was incessant watching to see that no
ready-used thread was introduced. Ladies when
not working would go and watch others to see that
all was fair.

"Once a lady, the wife of a secretary, was caught.
She had brought in wrapped about her waist a
great quantity of ready spun and dyed thread, and
she was caught with it. Such a sensation there was!
And when the queen was told she sent for the
culprit to be brought before her. The lady came,
very much ashamed at being caught, surrounded by
other ladies calling ' Fie!' at her. The queen
made an inquiry, and when it was clear that the

lady had really attempted to smuggle in the thread
the queen passed sentence upon her. The skein of
thread was to be hung round her neck and she was
to wear it till the morning as a badge of disgrace.

"So they hung the skein about her neck and it
fell over her bosom, and so she went away. She
was very much ashamed and cried at her disgrace,
but the other ladies only laughed at her. I was
quite sorry for her, but really there was nothing to
cry about, for it was all fun, Thakin.

"All night they worked dreadfully hard. The
thread was sized and then dried over hot fires and
woven and then dyed in a great hurry and dried
again over the fires. It was hard work, but it was
great fun all the same. And then next day there
was the glory of going in the procession offering to
the monks what you had worked hard all night
to make.

"It made one proud and happy.

"That was the festival of the full moon, the last
festival the palace ever saw, the last festival the
queen ever reigned over. Never shall I forget it.
Ah! Thakin, they were pleasant days, those in the
palace with the queen."

CHAPTER XX

THE GOVERNOR OF THE CITY

"All this time the air was full of rumours. I was but a child, how could I understand it all? There came a cloud hanging over the gayness of the palace, a cloud I knew not whence. But it was very visible and quickly growing more and more black. Even on those days and nights of rejoicing at the full moon we all felt that something was going wrong, that all was not as it used to be. The king was sad and the ministers were full of care. Only the queen seemed the same. If anything her eyes were brighter and she was prouder than before. When the days of the full moon were over it seemed as if we plunged at once into trouble and unhappiness. Many councils were held between the king and his ministers. Was the queen present the Thakin asks? Was the queen ever absent from the king? They lived and ate and slept and played together. They were hardly ever parted and never for long at a time ; half an hour, not more. What all the councils were about I cannot say. I heard much talk of a timber company cheating the king, and I heard of messages from the British government and then talk of war. Many soldiers came to the palace in those days and were sent forth in one direction and another. The king and queen gave them audience before they left, and the queen gave them presents, swords generally, with gold and jewels in the hilt.

" The governors of distant provinces came too. They were sent for I think by the king and they discussed many things. They talked of the men they could raise and the money and what arrangements should be made. I am a girl, Thakin ; girls do not understand those things. Talk of war frightens me. It is a horrible thing. I did not heed more than I could help.

" But otherwise things went on much the same in the palace. The king and the queen laughed and played with the maids of honour, the ministers came and consulted and went away again to do as they could, no one knowing much or caring very much.

" There was a curious thing happened just about that time.

" Trouble had broken out in the city. Thieves

wandered about at night and stole, robbers broke into houses and murdered and robbed. Men were getting restless everywhere, evil men scenting the trouble about to come and bestirring themselves. ' When the forest is on fire, the wild cat slaps his arm.'

" It was reported that these thieves and murderers were many of them natives of India and foreigners of sorts. I do not know if this was true or not, but it was natural now that we were quarrelling with the Indian government to suspect its subjects.

" Every one said it must be foreigners who were committing all these crimes and there was a great stir about it. Merchants came and petitioned the palace that their trade was being interrupted and they were losing money. Stringent orders were therefore sent to the governor of the city, the Myowun, that he must at once, at any cost, put an end to these disturbances. It was a disgrace, he was told, that this the capital of the great nation should be troubled at night by evil characters and robbers. He must bestir himself and stop it.

" However, the disturbances did not stop. Patrols were sent all over the city at night with strict orders to arrest every one found out after nine o'clock, headmen of wards were told that they must arrange for watches to be held and other precautions taken. But still though some of the evil doers were caught and severely punished crime did not stop.

" Then one day there came a petitioner to the queen. It was the wife of the governor of the city. She was a handsome woman, still young, with beautiful large eyes, and as she came into audience her eyes were full of tears. The king and queen were then in the little pavilion with the fountain in front, near the tower with the winding stairs, and the governor's wife came in and knelt. The queen knew of course who she was, for she had been maid of honour once and often came to the palace to talk to the queen, and indeed the queen liked her very much, so when she came in thus with tears in her eyes the queen was very sorry for her and asked what it was all about.

" Then the governor's wife told this story. The town, she said, was troubled very much with thieves and wicked men who went about at night and robbed. The traders barricaded themselves in their houses and had watchmen, and the poorer people lay awake all night in fear. This was a sad state of affairs, and the king in his great concern for his people has commanded the Myowun, the speaker's husband, to stop all this trouble at once. The Myowun reported to the king that he was trying all he could to catch these thieves, but still the thieving went on. Things were as bad as ever despite the governor's statements of what he did. Would the king and queen like to know how it was that the royal orders were not obeyed but that their people were nightly plundered by robbers?

"Then the queen told her to go on and tell the reason, and the governor's wife went on.

"'I am ashamed to tell the queen about it,' she said, 'it is shameful to my husband, shameful to me, that I should have to bring such a tale to the queen's throne. But this is the reason of it. My husband's love has left me and he has taken to himself a mistress. He has forgotten me who am his wife, given to him by her majesty the queen, and goes after a strange woman, a foreigner. Every night when he is supposed to be going about the city rousing the guards, watching over the peace, he is with her. He sleeps by her side while I, his wife, am alone, and robbers pass about the streets. These robbers are of her kin, foreigners, and so he does not wish to have them arrested and punished. That is the reason of it.'

"When the queen heard this she was very angry. The wife of the governor had been one of her maids of honour, one of us, and had been given to the governor in marriage by the queen not many

years before. And the queen hated to hear of
infidelity by husbands towards wives. That was
of all things the one that made her most angry.
So she turned to the king and proposed that the
governor should be immediately punished very
severely, perhaps executed if it were true.

"But when the wife saw how angry the queen
was I think she was afraid. She had gone too
far. She did not want her husband punished, but
only that his Indian mistress should be taken from
him. So that when the king agreed with the
queen that the conduct of the governor was such
as merited very severe notice, she began to plead
for him. If the king would but send for him and
warn him that would be enough. She did not
want him punished or dismissed. He was a good
servant to the king. It was this Indian woman
who had beguiled and bewitched him. If the
woman were banished and the governor warned
that would be enough. She pleaded hard before
the queen. For although the king's name came to
her lips it was the queen in reality.' She it was
who decided.

"When the queen had listened to what the
governor's wife said, she replied that due measures
would be taken. Inquiry would be first made, for
it would be improper to punish any one without

due inquiry. An investigation would be held, and if it were proved that the governor was behaving wrongly, the punishment meet for the offence would be imposed. It was very wrong, said the queen, for any husband to treat his wife so. To take a mistress was a scandalous thing, contrary to all law and religion, and she would never overlook such a thing.

"'See now the tears of the governor's wife,' she said to the princesses about her, '.because of her husband loving another woman. How much trouble and misery are caused to loving wives by the sins of their husbands!

"' Truly such an offence as this deserves punishment. When a husband has a wife how can he leave her for other women? It is only wicked men who can act so. Never will I permit such a thing. Wives must keep honourably to their husbands, and husbands to their wives, or I the queen will see to it.'

"The queen was very much in earnest, Thakin. She meant all she said and more. I do not know what the king thought of all this, whether he remembered a certain Shan princess. But he said nothing. The governor's wife could not say anything after the queen had thus passed orders and presently she went away.

"She was sorry, I think, that she had come. But she was in a passion then and did not think of consequences.

"It would have gone very hard with the governor if the queen had been allowed to have her way. An inquiry was made and I suppose it was proved that there was some truth in the wife's story, for the governor was arrested and put in gaol. He was put in leg-irons just like the other prisoners in the gaol, many of whom he had himself caused to be arrested. It would have gone hard with him, but that events then came so quickly one on the top of the other, and danger gathered so fast, there was no time to think of minor things. Perhaps the queen forgot. After fifteen days in irons in the prison the governor was released and reinstated."

"I should not think," I remarked, "that he felt very affectionate towards his wife on his release. Fifteen days in irons is not calculated to greatly increase one's love towards the cause of it."

"No, Thakin," she answered meditatively, "I suppose not. But she did not think. Women are very hasty."

CHAPTER XXI

THE COUNCIL OF WAR

"THE air grew fuller of rumours. There was to be war every one said. The British government did not like to see the timber company punished for its cheating and was about to make war because of them. The foreigners began to leave Mandalay and go down the river in the steamers to Lower Burma. A spy had come up from the British government to look about Mandalay and discover where it was weak and where it was strong. This was discovered just as he fled and the discovery made every one angry. The captain of the steamer who brought him up was arrested and tried and was sentenced to death for treachery.*

"There was great excitement everywhere. It was reported that there was a numerous British

---

* Captain Redmond, of the Irrawaddy Flotilla Company. He was kept till the taking of Mandalay, when he was released. He is now alive and well, still commanding on his steamer.

army collecting near the frontier to invade and attack us. Many steamers were engaged, it was said, to carry the troops. Then at last there came a final letter from the British government. It came up in a special steamer, and when it arrived there was a great excitement. The ministers were sent for from all about to come quickly to the palace to consider it.

" The king's council was held in the little white chamber that looks out on the courtyard where the water-tassel leaps. There is a daïs at one end of this, where the king and the queen sat, and below this were the ministers sitting on the floor. There were great mirrors about that chamber that gave back to you all the scene about you, mirrors at the sides, mirrors at the end of the chamber.

" The letter was read aloud by a secretary. I do not remember exactly what the letter said. How should a child remember all these things of state ? But it was to say that if the king did not do this and that and send an answer within so many days, then the English would make war upon him. One of the things was that nothing was to be done against the timber company, I remember. When it was finished every one was very angry.

" Then there was a discussion upon the letter— what was to be done ? Several of the ministers

THE KING AND QUEEN

spoke. The Taingda Mingyi wanted to have war. He was very angry at the letter.

"'Let the king declare war,' he said, 'against these foreign devils. Has not the king thousands of brave soldiers who can defeat these heretics and drive them into the sea ? Did ever any king hear such a demand as that made in this letter ? This company has been cheating the king, and after due and proper investigation by the proper court they have been found guilty and fined. And the king is ordered to set aside the orders of his court of justice and let these people off. For all this talk about another investigation is pretence. It is all talk. If the English have their way there will never be another investigation. This letter is full of words, but what it means is that the king is to become the slave of the English.

"'This "resident" they propose to send, he is to be the king. This is their way. Did not the English take the kingdom of Arracan and Pegu from the king's ancestors ? And now they are not content but must try to rob the kingdom of Ava. That is the meaning of such words.

"'But let the king make war. We have many brave soldiers and this war shall not be as the last. In this war the king shall be victorious. He shall drive the English from their places and reconquer these countries even as the great Alompra did. The king's army has been trained now as the foreigners' army has been trained. The palace is full of guns and ammunition. These English are but animals without faith or honour or religion as all the world knows. English faith is a byeword among the nations. Let the king make war.'

"He said a great deal more than this, Thakin, his words were full of wrath against your government.

" The queen was glad when the Taingda Mingyi spoke, for her mind and his were at one in this business. Indeed I think that many of those hearing were glad at the brave words of the Mingyi. They were angry at the letter and wanted revenge.

"Then the king turned to the Kinwun Mingyi and asked what he advised. 'What has the Kinwun Mingyi to say in this matter ?' And the minister bent forward and said,

" 'The letter is an evil letter. It' is difficult for the king to accept such a letter. It is full of insults and hard words. And it is true that the meaning of it all is that the English want the country. But still war is very difficult. I, the king's minister, have been to foreign lands, to India and France, and I have seen these armies of the English. They are very numerous and very well armed and savage. My lord's army cannot yet fight with them. Therefore let my lord keep the peace for yet a few years. What matters this resident and this company of timber traders ? They are wise men who can forget small things and remember great ones. Let the king forget these annoyances and remember his great kingdom. In a few years the army will be better trained and more numerous, and the king may have friends among the other nations. He can bide his time and strike when the blow will tell. But now it would not be wise to make war.

" ' If my king would send an answer to these English that their requests shall be fulfilled, then if indeed it be necessary to fulfil them, it can be done slowly, and meanwhile preparations can be made. In a few years there may be war, and success, but not now.'

" Such words said the Kinwun Mingyi, the cunning old minister whom King Mindon had made, trying to soften the wrath that the letter had caused. But it was all of no use.

" The other ministers were very angry and the queen was more angry than all. She had always hated the Kinwun Mingyi, although I think,

Thakin, that he helped her husband to his throne.
She hated him because he often gave advice contrary to hers. He was for going softly and carefully while the queen was always in a hurry. She
always hated him, and if he had not received from
the old king an order giving him assurance against
any form of death or punishment, she would, I
think, have tried to have him degraded long ago.
She was very angry, and as I sat behind her I
could see her shiver all over and her cigarette went
out because she breathed so fast she could not
smoke it, and she leant back for another. I rolled
it quickly and lit it and gave it to her, but it soon
went out and she forgot about it.

" The other ministers spoke too. I think they
all urged the king to make war. I think the
Kinwun Mingyi was the only one who wanted peace
at the council.

" They pressed for war and spoke of all the
preparations that were made. They spoke of the
Immortals of the king's guard, who were tattooed
with charms and made proof against bullets and
sword cuts, and that they could withstand the
English troops with ease and destroy them. They
told the king how a Chinaman had invented a
mirror with which the sun's rays could be reflected
on the enemy and his army utterly burnt up.

Many speeches were made. And whenever any one spoke of war and how the king would win, the queen's eyes brightened and she looked at him and smiled. Men were glad, Thakin, when the queen smiled at them. It meant many things in those days that the queen should be glad at a man's words.

"But the king sat still and silent and said nothing, nor smiled at all. I do not think he liked the idea of war, even successful war. He was a religious man, and had been told that all war is very evil. Such men should not be kings, Thakin.

"Great kings are those who are savage and cruel, delighting in ravaging other countries and killing the people, making the rest slaves. Great kings are those who rejoice in conquest and in the death and misery of others. They are robbers and murderers in high places. King Thibaw was not like this.

"So they all pressed the king to make war, and the talk went on from the time it would take the sun to sink from the zenith to yonder roof. It was a very long council.

"Then at the end the Kinwun Mingyi spoke again and advised the king to make peace. 'Did not one of my lord's ancestors make war and lose

Arracan, and another make war and lose Pegu ?
Let my king be advised, lest quickly he lose Ava
also.'

" The king's mind was bent towards the Kinwun
Mingyi. All those at the council could see that the
king was not agreeing with those who would have
war. He knew the Kinwun Mingyi was wise, and
his words fell into the king's mind.

" Then at last the queen spoke. After all the low
deep voices of the ministers her voice sounded
clear as a silver bell in the white chamber.

" ' I too, the queen, the king's wife, have something to say to the king upon this subject. Is my
king a servant of these foreigners that he should
suffer these things ? '

" She stopped for a moment, and when she went
on the words fell slowly from her lips as drops that
fall from a tree after rain.

" ' The Kinwun Mingyi has said that if the king
makes war he may lose his kingdom. Let it be
that this is true. Better it were to lose the Golden
Kingdom than to listen to orders like a slave. Is
my lord in his palace to be but as the governor of
a province, to do this and that at the bidding of a
greater than he ? My lord is a great king, and his
sword is sharp. He shall reply with its edge to
those that contemn him. Sooner shall we die with

our soldiers than live with chains of words about our necks. But all this talk of defeat is the talk of old men and cowards. There is no fear. The brave soldiers, the Immortals, shall soon conquer the enemy and drive him into that black sea whence he came, sea devil that he is. The Taingda Mingyi shall command, and all shall go well.'

"Then she turned from the king and looked at the Kinwun Mingyi, and her voice was full of scorn and hate.

"'As to the Kinwun Mingyi, he is old and afraid. He is not a man, a minister, but a woman, an old, old woman. Look, my maidens shall bring him even now a petticoat and a fan that he may dress as becomes his words, and when he goeth forth from the king's presence the world shall know him for what he is.'

"The queen stopped speaking and was silent. Her face flushed and her eyes were very bright, then slowly one by one tears came into her eyes and she put her hands over her face and cried. The tears ran down her fingers and dropped from her rings, and a sob came out of her throat. We were all very much afraid, for we had never seen her cry before, and it was terrible to see a queen cry in a council. The ministers were all bowed forward with their clasped hands before them on the rugs and their faces to the ground. Within the chamber all was still, but from without there came the laughter of the water falling into the basin and the cry of birds. Outside all was gay with sunshine and happiness, but inside it was still and sad as death.

"Only the king's eyes wandered to and fro, passing down the rows of ministers in their state dresses and white fillets till his eyes fell upon the Kinwun Mingyi, the wise old minister whom his father had honoured, whom his queen had dishonoured. Then he looked away through the pillars to the white courtyard where the sun was shining and the trees waving their green fingers to and fro. All the fate of the nation was in his thoughts.

"War or not war? Who was to prevail, the queen or the old minister?

"If he could only have seen into the future, Thakin, only have known a few days ahead. But all the looking across the gardens, even to the purple hills far away in the distance, could not tell the king what was to be in those next few days.

"His eyes came back from far away and fell upon the queen sitting there by his side on the purple cushions, and at last he spoke.

"'I have heard,' he said, 'what the ministers

have advised, and there seems to be no other way than war. Only by war can we save our kingdom from dishonour. But that all things be done in proper order, let there be now assembled a great council of ministers as the custom is. Let them meet as soon as may be, all the ministers whom custom orders, in the Byedaik, and deliberate on this subject as the law of the kingdom has always been. When the decision is made, orders will be issued.'

"Then the king rose from the daïs and turned towards his own apartments, and the queen followed and we followed the queen.

"I saw her face as she went, and it was quite white now, but her eyes were very bright. She looked glad and yet sorry. I looked back as we went out, and saw the Kinwun Mingyi going away. His face was sad and he was ashamed; but the other ministers were merry and jested as they went.

"Ah! Thakin, I shall always remember that council, but I cannot tell it you all word for word. How can a child remember everything? I forget many things and get confused sometimes.

"Thakin, you have seen how the wind is strong and the clouds are fleeing fast, the blue sky comes in glimpses now in one place now in another, shows for a moment till the clouds cover it up again. That is the way my memories come back to me. A scene, a word, a face, comes to me ; it stays but for a moment, and forgetfulness covers it."

CHAPTER XXII

FINAL STEPS

"So a great council was held in the Byedaik, a building on the north of the palace. To this council all the ministers above a certain rank were called, the Mingyis and the secretaries and the governors. Many ministers came to the great council. For it was the old custom of the state never to declare war without holding a great council and receiving its consent. It was the custom always to discuss serious questions of state in this council, and to take its advice upon all points.

"But of course the real ruler was the king. If he wanted to declare war he did so, but few kings would do so if their ministers disagreed.

"Messengers were sent everywhere to summon ministers to come to the council. They ran on foot through the city and on horseback to those who dwelt in the outer town and summoned them in haste to the palace, and they came up quickly, riding or in bullock carriages.

"The king and queen sat in the little garden pavilion and waited for news from the Byedaik. It was not the custom for the king to go there, but only to send his orders as to the question to be debated. It really did not matter very much, as it was only a matter of form.

"It was very hot that day in the gardens. The rains were over and the south-west wind had stopped and the north wind had not yet come. Not a leaf moved. The waters lay in the tanks like mirrors reflecting the green banks and the trees, without a broken ripple on them.

"No one spoke much. The king and queen sat side by side as they did always, and now and again the king would say something to the queen about the council or about the news from the frontier. But the queen did not answer much. She seemed to be tired with what had occurred that day.

"Presently the queen's mother, the Sinpyumashin, came round by the west of the palace to join the king and queen. She had two or three maids of honour with her, carrying her fan and betel box and cushion.

"She came to the pavilion and sat down beside the queen. 'We are waiting to hear the decision

236

of the council,' said the queen to her mother. 'You have heard that they are now discussing the answer to that letter from the foreigners.'

"The queen-mother said she had heard. 'I heard everything,' she said, 'what the Taingda Mingyi said and what the Kinwun Mingyi said and what you said, Su, Su. I am very sorry to hear it all.'

"The queen did not say anything, but looked at her mother and then looked at the king. There was a long pause.

"When the queen-mother came and sat down by the queen her maids of honour came up with her and found places beside us. One of them came and sat next to me. She was a Shan girl with such a fair face and pink cheeks. But she was not pretty because her face was round and chubby. Round faces are not pretty, but only long ones.

"I had never been near a Shan girl before, and I looked at her very curiously. Another girl was a girl I knew, whose father was a Chinaman in the king's service. I recognised her at once and tried to whisper to her, but she held up her hand. So I saw that the queen-mother was in a bad temper, and it was better not to try and talk to any one, or she might hear and be annoyed and we might get into trouble. I kept quiet.

"We waited and waited till the time seemed

dreadfully long. Afar off on the east of the palace
we saw through the trees that people were coming
and going continually. They were very busy
there. Once a cannon went rumbling out dragged
by elephants, and this reminded us of the war and
of the council that was going on, which I had
almost forgotten.

"Then at last we saw a herald coming through
the garden towards us. He came along fast, and
when he came to the pavilion he knelt down and
spoke.

" He spoke very loudly and very clearly, and he
used all the long and difficult words that people use
when they talk of state matters. I do not remember exactly what he said, but his meaning was
this :

" There had been held a great council, and all
the great ministers were there. He named them,
the Kinwun Mingyi and the Taingda Mingyi and
the Hlethin-atwinwun and the Myowun, and many
more. They had considered the affairs of state and
read the letter from the foreign government, and
many ministers had spoken. Some had spoken on
one side and some upon the other, and in the end
when all sides had been heard then each gave his
opinion. And the opinion of the great council was
this, that an evasive but friendly answer should be

sent to the foreign government. They did not think it would be wise to have war.

"Thakin, you never saw any one so angry as the queen was when she heard that message. The king too was annoyed. It was an unheard-of thing for the ministers thus to oppose an order of the king.

"The king had declared war, and the council, his council, declared for submission. The king was very vexed. If he had known beforehand that the majority of the ministers were for peace he too, perhaps, would have declared for peace. But now he had ordered war and he could not go back, could not say he was wrong and would change. War he had said and war it must be.

"When a weak man makes up his mind, Thakin, he is far harder to turn than a strong man.

"But if the king was vexed the queen was furious. 'See now, Maung, Maung,' she said, 'what sort of ministers yours are. You give them orders to declare war and they send you a message that they think peace would be better. Your father the great king would have executed or dismissed them.'

"And then the queen's mother interposed. 'Nay, but consider,' she said. 'This is a dreadful thing that you are bringing upon the country, that

239

the king who used to be a monk should declare for war, which is such a wicked crime. It will bring nothing but trouble, nothing but evil. And every one is against you. Even your own ministers are trying to save you. Consider, therefore, and be careful.'

"What the king would have replied to the queen-mother I do not know, but he had no time to speak. The queen turned upon her and spoke very fast, very angrily, 'What is the good of talking now?' she said; 'war is decided upon. It is no use to argue. And besides war is right.'

"But the queen-mother would not be so silenced. 'You are throwing away your throne,' she said. 'Who put you on the throne but me? Who plotted for the king and did all things for the king but me? And now that I see that throne about to be upset, shall I not speak?'

"But the queen would not listen. She was furious. She forgot that it was her mother who was there pleading to her, and she answered bitterly:

"'Whether you gave the king his throne or not, I do not know. But you understand nothing of these affairs. They are affairs of state that do not concern you or any one except the king.'

"'All who do know state affairs are against

you,' answered the queen-mother. 'There is your council, all the old ministers who are trained in business, they say that there should be no war. But you who are young think that you know better than the old ministers of the king your father, and you will have your way. There is the Kinwun Mingyi, why do you not listen to him ? '

" If the queen was angry before, she was twice as angry now. Listen to the Kinwun Mingyi, him whom she hated ? She turned her face upon her mother, and it was pale with anger, and her eyes shone and her hands trembled.

" 'The Kinwun Mingyi,' she answered slowly. 'Yes, you and the Kinwun Mingyi are a pair. You should be married, or go into a retreat together as hermits. You are a good match.'

" There was a dead silence. The queen was sitting, with her lips tight set one against the other, staring across at the palace. The king looked at the queen in dismay. Never had such words been used by a daughter to a mother. Though the king did not want to listen to her advice, yet would he never have spoken so to the queen-mother. It was terrible. But he was afraid to interfere.

" Then the queen-mother rose up from her place and went away without a word more. She went down from the summer-house and across the garden

to the west side of the palace, and then round to
the north, where her rooms lay, walking very
slowly. I did not see her face, but there were
tears surely in her eyes. It was a terrible thing to
see a mother leaving her children like this.

" We sat and looked at each other sideways in
turn, fearing we knew not what would come after
this. Never had the queen been so before.

" Suddenly the queen spoke to the king, cheer-
fully, brightly, with all the anger and bitterness
gone from her eyes.

" ' Maung, Maung,' she said, ' come let us go to
the palace. For orders must be given about this
war, and the matter must be settled at once and
the answer sent to the English. Let us go to the
palace and call the secretaries.'

" Then the king and queen arose and went
together to the palace. What the queen said, that
the king did. So the king and queen went to the
palace, and the ministers and secretaries were sent
for, and there was more consultation. But now it
was all about war. There was no more talk of
peace, for that was all decided and done for. War
was to be, and the only question was now about the
way.

" That day, and for many days after that, the
king was very busy with his ministers and secre-

taries. The answer to the English government was made and sent, and it said that the terms could not be accepted. They were impossible. And a proclamation was made out to issue to the people.

" War was declared, it said, between the king and the government of India. There would be fighting. But the people were not to be alarmed nor disturbed. Though there should be war, yet would they not be troubled. For the king had many troops, many brave and glorious soldiers, who would attack the heretic foreigners and drive them into the sea. Let the people, therefore, not concern themselves, but buy and sell, plough and reap, marry and perform their religious duties as they were wont. The king was a great king, and he would protect them. Such was the proclamation.

" Preparations were made too for the war. Orders were sent out to all the governors of the provinces to raise men and money and to assist in the war. Officials were sent down from Mandalay to the frontier. The river was to be blocked to stop the steamers, and forts were to be armed. Such a hurry there was all day long in the palace, men coming and going and orders being issued. On the south side of the palace in our gardens all was always quiet, but on the north side, where the arsenal was and the stores, men were at work all day long, and rifles and cannon were always being issued. Whenever we went round to the north garden we could see the work going on.

"The queen liked to go and watch the cannon and the guns being got ready. She took great interest in all these things. Whenever an officer left Mandalay to go to the frontier to command the troops the queen ordered him to come and see her before she went. And when he came she would talk to him and tell him to fight well for her and for the kingdom. She would give presents, too—a diamond ring, a gold-hilted sword—and tell him when in the fight to look upon these and remember the king and her. Great, she said, was the honour and glory due to the soldier who fought well for his country. The young officer would listen, and would swear to the queen that he would win, and would drive out the foreigner and rescue all those of their fellow-countrymen who were slaves on the lower province.

"Ah! Thakin, the queen knew how to make men faithful to her. She spoke to them so kindly and so sweetly; when he was young, and un-married, she promised one of the maids of honour as a wife when he returned.

" ' So be sure and fight well,' she said, ' and remember that there is awaiting you on your return honour and favour and wealth, and perhaps a wife.' Then the queen would laugh, and the young soldier would laugh too.

"Amongst others that were sent for by the ministers and ordered to take command here or there was my father. He was told that by great favour of the king he was appointed to command one of the gunboats on the river, the one called the *Bundoola*. He was to take charge of her and put her in fit order, and then go down to the frontier to join the other boats and destroy the English steamers.

" But, alas ! Thakin, when my father went to the steamer, he found it was all of no use. The boilers were rotten and the pipes broken and the guns jammed. Besides, he could get no money to make repairs with. He asked and asked, but it was of no use, and the steamer was never sent down. It would have been no good. That was the way of many things."

CHAPTER XXIII

THE OTHER SIDE

MEANWHILE in Lower Burma there was no indecision nor doubt. It had been decided by the government long before that it would be necessary to go to war with Upper Burma sooner or later. The execution of the king's sons in 1879 very nearly brought on the war, but the outbreak in Afghanistan caused it to be postponed.

Nevertheless, the plan of campaign had been carefully worked out, and preparations had for long been made for the eventuality. Long before it was known whether King Thibaw would accept or no the demands of the Indian government, troops had been brought over from India; warlike stores had been collected, and the expeditionary force which was to march on Mandalay had been organised.

The column that had advanced on Ava in 1825 had gone by land. It had marched wearisomely

246

through the roadless country on the left bank of the Irrawaddy, keeping with it a flotilla of boats that served as transport.

In the war of 1852 no column had entered Upper Burma. The Indian government had merely seized on Lower Burma, without caring to attack the king himself.

In 1885 other means were adopted. Since 1852 a great fleet of river steamers had been established on the Irrawaddy by the Irrawaddy Flotilla Company, steamers of small draft, capable of plying even in the dry weather, with considerable length and beam. These steamers, too, were able to tow a large flat on each side, and thus more than double the accommodation for troops and the tonnage available for transport of stores. It is only 400 miles by river from the frontier station of Thayetmyo to Mandalay, and as these steamers, even with the needful delays when carrying troops, cover sixty or eighty miles a day, it will thus be seen how much better in every way it was to proceed by river than by land. Many steamers were accordingly chartered for the conveyance of the troops and commissariat. One or two of these were armed with sixty-four-pounder guns to batter any forts that might be encountered, and others were fitted up for troops.

The force, which numbered about ten thousand men, assembled at Thayetmyo, and there awaited the day fixed by the ultimatum. When the steamer that was to bring the answer to the ultimatum came down empty, it was known that war was resolved on, and when, on November 9th, the letter from the Burmese government, refusing to comply with the demands of the Indian government, was received, all was ready for an advance.

The first reconnaissance into Upper Burma was made on November 14th, when a launch went up above the frontier and captured a Burmese government steamer, one of that mosquito fleet of which the *Bundoola* was a member. She was taken without fighting, save that an attempt was made to explode gunpowder on board her as she was taken. Being moored to the bank at the time with no steam up, she was an easy prize. How this story got changed on its way to Mandalay will be seen later. On November 15th the whole force crossed the frontier, and, moving slowly and cautiously, it came to Minhla on the 17th. Minhla was the frontier station of the Burmese government. There was a fort here on the right bank, a square structure of brick, which could be easily knocked into pieces by shells, and not much resistance was expected here.

But on the left bank some entrenchments had been laid out by the foreign engineers in the service of the king of Burma, and they were said to be well armed with artillery and manned by good troops. Consequently the main part of the column was landed on the left bank to attack these entrenchments, while a comparatively small detachment was landed to attack the fort.

The first attack succeeded completely. Instead of the completed, well-armed, well-manned works the troops expected to take, they found but half-finished ditches, with no artillery and but very few men, armed with wooden guns for the most part. The Burman skirmishers came out to meet their foe, and put up their guns at them, and put them down, and put them up again. It was merely playing at war like a child. The money which had been paid to buy rifles and good arms had been stolen, and wooden toys substituted. The army, which ought to have been fifteen thousand strong, was barely fifteen hundred unarmed villagers. Such was the queen's army, which was to retrieve her honour and to save the kingdom. Some of them were shot, and the rest ran away.

On the right bank a better resistance was shown to the Madras regiments which were landed to the attack. The fort held out bravely for a time against the assault of the troops and the battering of the big guns. Once or twice the assault failed. And then, at last, the door was smashed in by artillery and the place stormed. It was only a little place, and the commander died fighting to the end. Our loss was trivial. A force armed with artillery and breechloaders does not suffer much from a foe armed with flint-locks and wooden guns. Thus fell Minhla; so ended the only fight of the war.

Later on, when the people rose against us, they showed very different behaviour to this, though their arms were not much better.

After the victory at Minhla, the flotilla continued its way up stream, shelling a place now and again, but meeting with no resistance.

Proclamations were distributed by the general as he went, declaring that the war was only with the king and the government, and that if the people remained quiet no harm should come to them.

This assurance the people consider was violated when the country was afterwards annexed.

From Minhla to Myingyan is about three hundred miles or a little less, and the flotilla breasting the broad stream of the Irrawaddy took seven days to reach so far. It was on the 24th that they came to Myingyan, and with the big guns bombarded some entrenchments that lay above the town. It is necessary now to return to the palace.

CHAPTER XXIV

THE KING'S FOREIGN MERCHANTS

"That council Thakin, was the end of all our pleasant life in the palace. A little longer it went on, but it was never the same again. All the joy and gaiety were gone out of it. All the remainder of the reign of the king and queen was as one of those days when the rains are coming on; when far away down in the south the lightning is playing in the heart of a dense cloud, when the air is heavy and still, and the beasts are going to shelter. Overhead the sky is still blue, the sun still shines, but the thunder moans now and again and gusts of wind come whirling by, full of warning. So it was in Mandalay.

"The king and queen still reigned, the ministers held councils, and the business of government went on much the same as ever. But the air was full of fear and of rumours. People knew that away down there in the south events were taking place

252

which would change everything. Those who rejoice in trouble and reap their harvest during times of war came forth boldly; but those who like peace were afraid and hid.

"Business came almost to a standstill, many there were to sell, but who was there to buy, never knowing what might happen to him and to his goods? Merchants and traders kept their money and put it in safe places; many of the foreign merchants fled to Lower Burma, those who were left made their houses into strong places of defence and collected there in companies. Everywhere was suspicion and doubt. The foreigners feared and doubted the people of the city, that if any trouble came they would arise and burn the houses and loot such property as they could come by. The Burmese looked with suspicion upon the preparations of the foreign merchants.

"'Surely,' they said to each other, 'these men are plotting. Why else should they barricade their houses and prepare weapons and stores of food? They are plotting against the government.'

"One afternoon, I think it was the very next day after the great council of the Byedaik, a minister came and sought audience of the king. He was not either of the Mingyis, but another minister, one who had much power, but not so

much as they had. He came in to the king as he
was sitting in his rooms in his palace. The queen
was with him, of course, and I too was there sitting
behind the queen. They talked of one thing and
of another, of the news from the frontier and of the
troops going down there, and presently the minister
began to speak of the city. It was in a bad state,
he said. Notwithstanding the efforts of the officials the city was much disturbed. Men were
afraid and trade was stopped, and there was much
talk and many strange stories were current. There
was an absurd idea abroad that the foreigners were
gaining some success on the frontier.

"All the trouble, said the minister, was clearly
attributable to the foreigners who lived in Mandalay.
It was because of foreign timber traders that the
quarrel between the two governments had arisen.
And now the foreigners in Mandalay were spreading
all sorts of tales against the king and the government.
They seemed to have no confidence in the king.
They were even barricading the brick houses which
they had built. They pretended that they were
afraid of robbers, but no doubt the truth was that
they were plotting against the king. Probably they
were about to raise an insurrection in the city.
They were quite capable of such a thing. And
then the minister recommended to the king to

arrest the foreign merchants and execute some of them as traitors to the king. So spoke the minister, and because he was an old and well-tried servant of the king the king listened to him, but as the minister went on the king's face grew more and more disturbed, almost as if he was angry. It was quite strange to see the king like this, sometimes before he had been sad and troubled, but never angry. I thought he was agreeing with the minister about the foreign merchants, and was angry against them. All of us thought to hear him pass some order against them at once. I think even the queen thought so, for she never interfered at all, never said a word, just awaited the king's reply. Then the king answered the minister.

" 'I have heard what you have to say,' he said, 'I have heard and I have considered. It is shameful that counsels such as these are should be brought to me. The minister wishes me to arrest and execute my foreign merchants. But indeed such an act would be a disgrace. For what have these men done ? They have done nothing. They are afraid and hide in their houses and make them strong because of fear, because my officials do not govern the city well. Is that a thing to arrest them for ? They are the guests of the king in his city, and shall meet with all protection and all care.

They shall not be imprisoned, but shall be encouraged. If they rebel are we not strong enough to put it down at once? It would be indeed an unseemly thing if the king were afraid of a few foreign merchants in his city. But they will not rebel, they are afraid, that is all.'

"Thakin, the minister was very much surprised when he heard the orders of the king. He came thinking to please him with his foresight, and the king turned upon him like this. The minister was much ashamed, and crouched lower and lower as the king went on. The queen too was surprised, and looked at the king with raised brows as if she had never seen him before like this, as if this was a new spirit come to the king. All of us were surprised to see the placid king so excited.

"The king was not contented with rebuking the minister for his advice and with repudiating his proposals. When he had finished with the minister he paused a few minutes thinking, and then he turned to a secretary and gave an order.

"'I desire,' said the king, 'that all the foreign merchants be summoned to the palace. Write an order to the Myowun to warn them all to come. They are not to be afraid, but are to come in full confidence that the king wishes them nothing but good, and will take care that no evil befals them.'

"Next day the audience was held in the great glass chamber. The foreign merchants were brought there, and when they were all assembled the king and queen walked there from the little white pavilion, and we followed behind.

"They were a strange sight, Thakin, those foreign merchants. All kinds were there, Europeans and Indians, and men from Turkey and many other places. There were all sorts of faces, round and long, bearded and smooth, all tints from white to very black indeed. And they wore many kinds of dress, but none so gay as our dress. They looked a sad crowd indeed compared to what a crowd of our people would be, and they sat awkwardly as if not accustomed to that way of sitting. Many of them seemed very nervous as not knowing why they were called here. A speech was read to them by a secretary, a speech that the king had made ready before. This is what the speech said :

"'The king of Ava, of all white elephants, king of kings, and ruler of the universe, to his foreign merchants. We have heard that the foreign merchants are disturbed, that they are afraid of what may come about, and that they are hiding in their houses from fear. And so we the king have sent for our foreign merchants to tell them to be of good courage. If there be war between the king and any foreign power that is not a matter to alarm the merchants. That is a question of governments and soldiers.

" ' There will be fighting, no doubt, but it will be far away. No one shall hurt the merchants of the king. Let them forget that there is war. Let them trade as before, buy and sell, and go hither and thither trading, and think only of that. As they were wont to act before let them act now.

" ' And if there arises any difficulties in any matter, who shall put that right but the king? Whatever the merchants require let them tell the king, and he will see to it. The king has been told that the merchants are in difficulties because the trading steamers have ceased running. Let them be of good heart about that.

" ' If the company's steamers will not run, then will the king see to it. His own royal steamers shall take their place, and run up and down the river. For steamers are necessary that trade be carried on properly. The king will command his officials to see to this.

" ' Let the merchants consider what they require,

and tell the king, being sure that he will listen to them. Evil men have brought the king reports against his foreign merchants, but the king has not believed them. Let them be sure that he will not believe any reports against them, but will protect them always, as is the duty of kings.'

" Thakin, I think that was his own speech. I think that, of all the acts done under his rule, that was the only one he did himself. For those were his own words. Not the words of the queen or of the ministers, but his own thoughts. He was always kind and good tempered, hating to see any one troubled or in danger, and for this once he spoke for himself. He might have been even a good king in time if he had remained to grow old.

"When the merchants heard the speech they seemed to be all very pleased, and they cried out at the goodness of the king, and thanked him for his mercy extended to them. After some more speaking, they went away.

"All this audience the queen sat by the king, but said nothing. I do not know whether she agreed with the king or not ; perhaps she did not care very much. Perhaps she saw that it was a kingly thing to do, and would bring honour to the king, and could do no harm. But I do not think

259

she would have done it herself. She would not have allowed the execution, but she would not have sent for the merchants to make them a speech.

"The merchants went away lauding the greatness of the king, and none of them were ever hurt, either themselves or their property, as long as the king was in power. He kept his promise to them, and no one dared to disturb them or injure them after the king had spoken his orders so firmly.

"But you cannot stop a storm with words. The lightning and the rain care nothing for all these; and all the people saw the storm coming up the river. All, I think, but the queen, who could not but believe that she and her king were stronger than any storm. The storm came nearer, and the people were more and more afraid.

"My mother came now and again to see me, and said that my father and many others of the people were blockading themselves in their houses, and making plenty of provision of food and arms, fearing outbreaks in the city.

"Thakin, when I look back, that time seems to me longer than all the time besides that I spent in the palace. And yet it was but twenty days. From the beginning to the end not more than

twenty or twenty-one days came and went. But
they were as long as a bad dream, that takes you
through years of trouble, in what, if you were
awake, would be but a moment of time."

CHAPTER XXV

WHAT NEWS?

" THE first news of the war that came to the palace was of a fight between the king's steamers and some English steamers below Minhla near the frontier. A messenger came with news from there for the council, and it was said that there had been a great fight and many men killed, but that in the end the king's ships had been victorious and two English steamers were taken.

"You know, Thakin, and I know now, that this was not true, that it was a mere pretence of the commander of the frontier to prevent the bad news coming to the palace, which would perhaps have caused him to be dismissed or even punished. But every one in the palace heard it and believed it. The queen herself told us of it, and was very glad, thinking it was the beginning of many victories.

"That night a great pwè was ordered in the palace on account of the victory. It was held as

262

usual in the great porch before the southern face of the palace. The king and queen and princes and ministers sat upon the space before the large audience-room with the glass panels. The dancers danced below ; and around them in the great portico were all the lower people of the palace, the soldiers and the servants and followers, many hundreds of them, I think. As you sat up on the high place you looked down and saw the open circle where the dancers danced, and then a great sea of faces all around them ; from the children sitting on the ground in the inner row to the men standing in rank behind rank, away into the gardens even. The lights under the portico were so bright that outside the night seemed very dark. It was as if the dancers were held in a great ring of faces and the faces held in a ring of night closing and pressing them in.

"It was a great pwè, and the actors in the play made speeches on the greatness of the king and queen and the value of their armies. They laughed at the foreigners, and at the idea that they could come and do any hurt to the kingdom. The great and brave army of the king would soon drive them away into the sea and the kingdom be restored as it was in the days of Alompra.

" It was very beautiful to see the dancers dancing, dressed in wonderful dresses of silver and of gold that the queen had given them. The best dancers and singers and the most beautiful women were there acting before the king and queen that night. Down where they danced it was very bright with the torches and lamps ; but where the king and queen sat there were not many lamps, only you could see the diamonds glitter around the queen's neck, and the golden bangles shine as she moved.

"When the best actress had danced, and had sung a beautiful song to the queen of how great and gracious she was, like the full moon beside the king her sun, and how the people loved and feared her, and how the foreigners were like the night that wished to darken the kingdom, the actress was called to come to the queen. So she came from out the circle to the steps that led up to the place where the queen sat, and there she knelt down.

" The queen ordered that it should be said to her that she had sung well, but that 'soon there would be more to sing of than the capture of little ships. When Rangoon was taken and the foreigners driven out and the Burmese of the lower country made again free men, that would be something to sing about. Let the actress consider what she

THE PORCH WHERE THE PLAY WAS HELD

would sing then. If her song was beautiful now, why how much more must it be beautifu then?

"A maid of honour, one of the oldest maids, who was not shy, then came forward and repeated in a loud voice so that all the people could hear what the queen had said. And she gave to the actress a beautiful gold bracelet with jewels in it that the queen took from her arm to give the actress.

"When all the people round saw the bangle and heard the gracious words of the queen a murmur ran through them as when the wind blows in the trees.

"The king too gave a present to the chief actor and money to be divided amongst the other actors; and all night long the music sounded in the palace; the music sounded and the actors sang and the people laughed, till at length, far away, you could see the summits of the Shan Mountains black against the dawn.

"No one slept all that night in the palace, for they were drunk with the beginnings of victory. They had their fill of rejoicing that night; no one ever rejoiced again. No more were any victories reported, there were no more pwès in the palace. That was the last dance the king and queen ever saw—ever shall see—for I fear there are none to amuse them, Thakin, in their prison across the far water.

"After all that was confusion. More messengers came—messengers were always coming—but there was no certainty to be made out of the reports they brought. Sometimes they spoke of victory and said that the foreigners were being defeated and driven down the river, sometimes that the foreigners were ascending the river. But they were only being allowed to ascend the river so as to be more severely defeated. When they had come up a certain way the river would be blocked behind them and they would be entirely destroyed. I cannot say, Thakin, whether the ministers received true reports, or not ; I can only speak of what we heard, of the rumours that flew from lip to lip about the palace.

"Then, after a day or two, the rumours became all of one kind—that we had been severely defeated, and that the foreigners were pressing on up the river. Every one heard these rumours, and faces looked sad and frightened. All faces looked sad but the queen's. She never spoke of defeat, but of victory, always of great success and of victory.

"The foreigners were being destroyed and the armies of the king were successful everywhere.

Why did we look sad ? she asked ; and because none of us dared to tell the queen of the rumours that were spread about, we pretended not to be sad, but glad. We must rejoice, she said, because of the good news of the armies. How much of the truth the queen knew I cannot tell, whether the ministers told her of all they knew, or whether they were afraid to do so. But whatever she knew, she was always very cheerful. When she was with the king she was always happy and confident, and spoke to hm merrily of how they would go in state to Rangoon when it was conquered and see the ships and the great sea. Indeed, Thakin, she went there very soon and saw the ships and crossed the sea as she said she would, but how differently to her thoughts—ah ! how differently !

"But Mebya had doubts I am sure. She did not know what was true. Behind all her smiling face and happy manners she was very much afraid that things were not right. For see, now, what she did. One morning early the queen went out to walk in the gardens on the north of the palace, and she called only one maid of honour, myself, to follow, and forbade the rest ; so I went behind her with the golden box of tobacco and the cigarette papers. These were the gardens where we used to play at hide-and-seek with the king and queen in those days which were but yesterday, but already appeared long ago.

"There were canals there in the south gardens and ponds of water, and long avenues of trees that wound to and fro, and you crossed the canals by narrow foot bridges and climbed up little hills where there were rocks and ferns. It was very cool there in the early morning in November when the mist hung like a veil upon the water, and the flowers were covered with dew, and the queen was fond of walking there along the canals and watching the fish swim to and fro. As you stood in the gardens you could see the palace so beautifully through the trees, the palace with its red and golden walls, and the carved roofs of the audience-chambers, and, above all, the great spire gleaming in the early sunlight and sending out a myriad sparkles from the mirrors let into the gilding.

"Beyond these gardens at one end is the white Boddhi pagoda, and some open ground where the children of the palace officials used to play. The queen went to this end, walking slowly under the trees, and stopped behind a great tamarind trunk and beckoned me to her side; and she looked beyond, and there were many children playing by the water, running and laughing; some of the boys playing football. Then she ordered me to go and

THE PALACE GARDENS

call one of the children to come to the tamarind
tree, but not to say the queen was there. I
went and called a little girl I knew about eight
years old, the daughter of one of the secretaries,
and the child came with me and took my hand,
and we went to where the queen was standing
alone, behind the tamarind tree in the shadow.

"When the little girl saw the queen she was
much afraid and wanted to run away, but I told her
there was no fear, that the queen only wished to
give her a present because she was such a pretty
little girl, so the child stood with me before the
queen.

" Then Mebya the queen told me to ask the
child what she heard her parents talking about in
the evenings before the lights were lit, and I coaxed
her, and she said that her father and mother talked
of the fighting, and how our soldiers had run away,
and that the foreigners had taken a fort down the
river and killed many of our people, and were
advancing up the river.

"She also said that her parents talked last
night that it would be necessary to bury all their
gold and silver, and that her mother had told her
she must give up her gold bangles to be buried, for
that wicked foreigners were coming to Mandalay
and would steal them all.

" You will understand, Thakin, that the child did not tell it all like this, but bit by bit ; with coaxing and care she told all she knew, and she cried a little at the end, partly because she was afraid of the queen, and partly because of having to give up the golden bangles that foreigners might perhaps steal.

"While little Ma Than was speaking the queen did not say anything. She only listened, and as she listened her face grew whiter and whiter and her eyes larger. When the child had finished the queen gave her a gold jewel from her wrist and bade her tell no one of what the queen had asked her, only to say that the queen called her and gave her a jewel. So little Ma Than ran back to her friends very pleased and delighted with the present the queen had given her ; and I called another.

"Altogether I called four children, and they all told the queen the same, that their parents talked only of defeat and loss, and two said that their parents were going to run away from Mandalay when the foreigners came in a few days.

"When they had finished the queen went away slowly, and I followed her. As she left the tree she said to me: 'Thou hast heard what the children have said. They are too young to have learned to lie. It must be all true. It is the ministers and generals who dare not tell me the truth. But thou who hast heard what they say, forget it, and dare not to speak to any one of it.' Then she went down the garden, and she looked so sad, ah, so sad!

" It is terrible, Thakin, that when an enemy is advancing to destroy a great kingdom the queen can only hear the truth from children, who are too young to have learned how to lie. Of all the ministers and generals she had raised into power, of all her thousand servants whose lives lay in her hands, there was not one to tell her truly of the ruin coming up the river. They were afraid of her, Thakin.

"She had forced on the war believing her army was a good army, her ministers honest men, her generals brave and experienced soldiers. Some of the ministers tried to save her from making war, but she would not. And now they were afraid to tell her of the disaster she had brought on the kingdom. There was no one now who dared to tell her the truth, who even cared to tell her.

" She, the great queen, who had through her husband the king ruled the Burmese nation and the Shan princes, who had sent hundreds to death and given to hundreds power and wealth, whose palace was full of gold and silver and precious stones, had no one to help her in her trouble. I was only a little girl, Thakin, and I could not understand so well then as I can now, looking back; but I was very sorry for the queen.

"The queen walked back through the arches of the trees, and near the west entrance she saw the king come out and go towards the garden pavilion. When she saw him she walked quickly and came up to him, and asked him aloud if there were any new victories of the troops reported that morning. Her voice sounded gay and she laughed, and all the sad look had gone from her face."

CHAPTER XXVI

SURRENDER

"So we went on for a day or two, the news always growing worse and worse, till at length no one tried to hide what it was. There was consternation everywhere. The foreign maids of honour had left, and also many of the other maids. There was so much fear of the foreigners who were coming up the river that fear of the king and queen grew less, and people did things that a month ago they would never have dared to do.

"Still, there were some who kept a good heart, or at least pretended to do so, and the queen looked always happy and smiling when in public with the king. For she was of great courage. Till at last something happened that made it no longer of any use to even hope that things would turn out well.

"After the queen had been into the garden talking to the children, I was ill with fever, and could

not go to attend upon her. I lay in my room sick
and hot, and my mother, when she heard I was
sick, came to the palace to attend to me, and I
heard but little of the news that went on. It was
one morning, and I was in my room, and my
mother was stroking my head because I had a
headache. Suddenly there was a great commotion
and the noise of people running to and fro and
talking. My mother went out to see what it was,
and left me alone. I was afraid, because I was
sick, and could not go out and see what the matter
was. I thought there must be some terrible news
come, or some catastrophe happened in the palace,
or a rebellion. I dragged myself to the window,
and, looking out upon the gardens, I could not see
any one there, for the day was hot ; a strong wind
was blowing up from the south right into my
window ; and, as I stood there and listened at the
window, there came on the breeze a low, soft
sound, like thunder far away in the mountains, and
after a minute it came again and again. I did not
know what it was. I could see no thunder-storm ;
the sky was blue, with little white clouds flecked
across it. There was no sign of any thunder. I
could not make it out, and my head was too heavy
to think, so I went back from the window and lay
down again, and soon my mother came in. I

asked what the trouble was, and said I had looked out of the window, but could see nothing. My mother said, 'Did you hear no sounds?' and I said, 'Yes; a sound as of thunder far away.' Then she told me it was the great guns of the English firing down the river.

"There was no doubt what it was, and there was terrible confusion in the palace. I suppose the king and queen knew that the foreigners were then close by, coming up. By that time it had become too late to conceal anything, and it was known that the steamers and soldiers of the Indian government were near by.

"To be told in words is one thing, Thakin; to hear with your own ears the thunder of their guns is very different. You may believe the words, but when you hear the cannon, *then you know*. I was very much afraid myself when I heard that the noise was the guns of the enemy. My fever seemed to get better, and I got up and dressed. My mother wanted me to go with her at once, and leave the palace, but I would not. I wanted to see the queen again, and not leave her yet. For I could not run away, as many of the maids of honour had done, and leave the queen after all she had done for me. So I rose and joined my company, which was waiting upon the queen.

" I found there was a council taking place. The
king was there, of course, and the queen, and as
many of the ministers as could be called in a hurry.
And it was decided very quickly to send down
messengers to tell the English general to stop ;
all would be agreed to if only the army would
stop. So the ministers counselled, and the king
agreed. But the queen said nothing. Surely it
was a bitter thing to her to have to submit like
this. But she saw it was all at an end. The
enemy was at the gate, and there was no hope
now of successful war. The only chance was to
submit.

" ' The last time the English came up,' said the
Kinwun Mingyi, ' when the king agreed to terms
they stopped their army, even though it was as
near Ava as the present army is near to Mandalay.
They stopped their advance, and returned to their
own country. It will be the same now. Let us
therefore send at once to the English general, and
say that all demands will be fulfilled, and that he
and his army can return.'

" So two ministers were sent off in swiftly
paddling boats down the river to meet the English
fleet. And in the palace, though there was humiliation, yet also there was the peace of knowing that
all was ended. The English army would return, and

the strain would be over, and if the terms were bad, well, it could not be helped.

"The council was very soon over, and the ministers sent away. There was nothing more to do, only to wait until the answer came. It was next day in the evening that the answer came. Ah, Thakin! such an answer. For the English general would not agree, would not stop, would not return.

"He would make no terms. 'Tell your king,' he replied to the ministers, 'tell your king that I am coming to Mandalay. If he wants peace then let him make peace at once. Let him surrender and tell his soldiers to surrender. Then will he gain the best terms. But no promises will be given.'

"Then, Thakin, was held the last council of the king. It was held as was the first council, in the same room, and with the ministers there just the same. But what a difference! Then all was pride and now all was humiliation, and only seventeen days between the two. In seventeen days all this had come to pass.

"The ministers who had been to see the English general gave their message. A month ago no one would have dared to bring such a message to the king, and even now the ministers were greatly ashamed, greatly afraid, at telling such a message. But it could not be helped, and so it was told.

"Then came a great dispute in the council. As before the war there had been two sides so were there now. As before the Kinwun Mingyi wished peace and the Taingda Mingyi war, so it was now.

"'Let the king surrender,' said the Kinwun Mingyi. 'Let him surrender and await the arrival of the English. For yet all may be well. They are a great people, and they will be merciful. They will make great demands, and we shall have to grant them. But still all may be well. It is better to trust them than to fight and lose, and fight and lose again, till all be gone.'

"But the Taingda Mingyi would not hear of this.

"'Never surrender,' he said. 'Fight, and fight, and fight. What if you have lost a little? That is nothing at all. We have not yet begun. What if the English are near Mandalay? they have come by water, they have no foothold on the country. What if they take Mandalay? the king can go to Shwebo, where the great Alompra lived. That is not near the river where steamers can get at it. I say let the king fight.'

"But ah! Thakin, the other ministers were against him. They were on the side of the Kinwun

Mingyi. For the king, what did he know of fighting? He had been a monk, and since he became king had lived all his days playing in the palace. What sort of fight could he make? Only the queen agreed with the Taingda Mingyi. She would have fought. If she had been king there would have been no surrender. But they were all against her, even the king. Her power lay only in her influence over him, and it was shaken. For it was she who had forced on the war, and now see what had happened. She had begun even to distrust herself, so that her speech was not so strong nor so assured as before.

"That was a sad council, that last council in the palace. Men spoke in low voices as if they feared the spirits that lived in the palace, in the throne, and in the great pillars might hear.

"It was a long council because there were long silences when no one spoke at all. It was almost dark when it was finished. The shadows were gathering in the great chambers about the tops of the pillars and in the far-away recesses. And when it was all over and the message sent to the English general and all orders given the king and queen rose and went out into the gardens. Far away in the west a scarlet sunset hung, and the air was odorous with the coming night.

THIBAW'S QUEEN

"The queen waved to us to keep behind, and we fell back. Then in the dark the king and queen walked to and fro and talked to each other in broken sentences, and when we returned to the palace we saw that there were tears in their eyes."

CHAPTER XXVII

THE LAST DAWN

"ALL that night we slept little from fear. For the English were coming, and who could tell what might happen? There was great unrest and fear. There were innumerable rumours. But we could only sit and wait. Nothing could be done, nothing but wait till they came. Nearly all day the king and queen just sat and looked at each other and were silent.

"Then in the evening we heard that the English would come next day, next morning. All that night I lay awake wondering and fearing. What would happen, what would happen? All that night no one slept in all the city and palace of Mandalay. The city was full of disturbances, sometimes shots were fired, and sometimes there were great shouts, and here and there the sky was lurid with a fire.

"I was weary of lying awake and thinking,

thinking, and I was glad when my room mate came and called me to go and attend upon the queen. So I dressed and went. She was sitting there in one of the rooms looking out into the garden, where it was yet dark. The king was not there, but the queen-mother was beside the queen.

" Since the meeting in the summer-house the queen had not spoken to her mother, but now in their desperate trouble they came again together. They sat in front of us looking out into the garden, and they wept and put their arms about each other, and now and then they said something to each other.

" 'What is it they say?' asked the maids of each other. 'Can you hear?' But no one could hear. Then the maids told me to keep near and listen.

" And I being a child crept near in the dark and listened to what they said. 'Seven years as seven days. Seven years as seven days.' That was what mother and daughter said to each other over and over again. 'Seven years have been as seven days.'

" So they watched the last dawn come. Far away behind the great Shan mountains the morning came clear and fresh, a spring of silver light. The silver turned to gold, and the gold to pink and crimson. We watched it slowly growing brighter in the gardens, brighter and brighter, and at last a long golden finger shot across the sky and fell upon the palace spire, kindling it into a flame. The beams came lower and lower till all the world was full of light. The birds called in the garden so merrily as they flitted from tree to tree, the fish leapt in the water-tanks, the flowers opened their hearts to the day. We watched it all sitting there, knowing we should see it no more, our seven years had gone as seven days.

" Once the queen spoke to us and told us we had better leave the palace soon, before the troops came. 'Who can tell what may happen,' she said, ' when those soldiers come ? I should be sorry that any harm should come to any of my maidens. You must go each to her home, those who have any other refuge must take it, for no longer can I give safety here. Any place will be better than this. But those who have not must stay with me, and I must stay with the king.'

" We did not want to go, Thakin. Those who had not cared to stay had already gone, but we who had stayed wished to stay still. And so we prayed to the queen to let us be with her.

"But she would not. We must go, she said, such of us that could, and she named us, for she knew us all. As soon as the troops were reported to be arriving at the landing-place we must go.

"When the queen gave an order no one could answer or disobey, so I said nothing, but my throat choked with sorrow. For I loved the queen.

"It was just after breakfast-time, about an hour or so before midday, that a report spread through the palace that the Indian government steamers were come. A messenger came and brought the report to the queen. And when she heard it she rose from where she was sitting and passed through the corridors and chambers till she came to the little courtyard below the round tower, where the look-out is, the same which my father built.

"A sentry was always kept on the top of that tower night and day watching. For from there you can see all the country. You look over the walls of the palace into the city, and over the great walls that surround the city, to the country far beyond. You can see right away to the foot of the Shan mountains on the east and north and south, till the country melts into purple distance.

WATCH TOWER

And you can see to the west over the crowded outer town right away down to the river, the great Irrawaddy, two miles broad and more, flowing between Mandalay and the grey Sagaing hills.

"We all followed the queen as she came to the courtyard, and we looked up and saw the sentry looking towards the west, looking as if he were watching. The queen ordered Ma Shwe Hmin to call to the sentry, and she called. The sentry looked down and the queen ordered to ask him what he could see, and the maid of honour asked. The sentry answered that he could see the steamers of the enemy coming up the broad reach that leads to the Mandalay landing-place. There were many steamers, he said, and they came on fast.

"The queen waited and ordered that the sentry should call down from time to time what he saw. Presently the sentry said that the steamers were making fast at the landing-place, and that crowds of the city folk were watching them. The queen asked if there was any firing and the sentry answered 'No.'

"Quickly, as the news spread through the palace, secretaries and others came thronging to the courtyard to hear, and there was a great crowd; but near the queen was an open space where no one dared to come save we who were attending on her. I do not know where the king was. I had not seen him that morning.

"There was a long wait, and the queen asked again if the sentry saw anything. Then the sentry answered that he saw troops landing—soldiers with horses and cannon, and still more soldiers—and that they were beginning to march up the long straight street that leads to the city gate.

"When the queen heard this, that the foreigners were indeed marching through the streets to the golden city, she realised that all was lost. Perhaps before this she had some little hope; many things might happen, but now all was lost. The golden kingdom of Ava was destroyed and the king and queen with it, and who could tell what would happen when these troops came to the palace?

"Suddenly she threw herself upon her face on the white pavement, and her hair fell about her face and she wept. When the people saw this they all went away, and there was no one left in the courtyard but the queen and ourselves.

"The queen rose upon her knees and beat her breasts with her hands, and cried aloud that she only had brought ruin upon the king and the country. 'It is I—I alone—I the queen that have brought destruction to the king my husband and my

"SUDDENLY SHE THREW HERSELF UPON
HER FACE"

people. It is I—I alone.' And again she threw
herself upon the white pavement and beat it with
her hands, and her whole body shook with sobs.

"We did not know what to do, Thakin. We
were all heart-broken to see the queen thus, but
what could we do ? Half as long as it takes a pot
of rice to boil she lay there upon the flags of the
courtyard, but it seemed like a year.

"Even so, Thakin, shall I last remember my
queen, even so, lying in the courtyard, mourning
for her vanished kingdom and her ruined king.

"Then at last she rose, and a maid of honour
knotted up her hair and arranged her disordered
dress, brushing off the dust, and she turned to go.
But as she turned she remembered. She remembered us, her maids, and spoke to us.

"'The foreigners,' she said, 'are upon us. You
have just time to escape from this palace where
misery has come. I have told you to go, go then
quickly, that my sorrow be not increased by any
trouble to my maids.' She waved her hands and
went away with the few maids of honour who
remained to her.

"We watched her go past the little white
pavilion, past the fountain where the water still
leapt, till she disappeared in the inner chamber
of the palace. She went to have her tears washed

away and jewels put about her neck and arms, that she might appear before her conquerors the queen she was. She vanished from our sight, and there was a long pause. And then we all dispersed."

CHAPTER XXVIII

VÆ VICTIS

" I WENT to my room and found my mother waiting me there, and very hurriedly I put my things together to go.

" Then, with a man behind us with my things, we went out. There was no trouble getting through the gate now, the guards hardly looked as we came up and asked that the gate be opened. They were talking amongst themselves in great excitement at what should be done.

" We passed through and the gate shut behind us for ever. Four years I lived there in the palace with the queen, such years as I shall never live again, years when I was very young and everything was so beautiful. I have never been near the palace since. How can I bear to go and see the places where the queen lived turned into other uses ? I see the spire afar off as I go on the steamer up and down the river, never shall I

289

want to see it nearer. Our palace shall remain in my memory fresh and beautiful for ever, girt about with its strong walls, guarded by its guards. It shall be to me always as when I knew it—the dwelling of a king.

" All the city within the gates was quite still as we passed through it. There were crowds of men gathering here and there sadly and sullenly, but there was no talk. We crossed the city and passed the great gates and over the drawbridge across the moat. The gates were open, no one was caring for them. The orders had been given to leave them open for the foreigners to enter. When we came across the moat we heard a curious sound like rippled thunder coming up the street. We could not make it out, but were afraid and ran into a house. We looked out from the verandah and saw the English soldiers come along, each man putting his foot to the ground at the same time as the others. That was what made the sound. They went along tramp, tramp, and the people looked at them in silence. They were very hot those soldiers and their faces were red. There were many of them. They came and came, and some passed into the city, and some went round north, and some went south, marching along by the moat."

I will just add a few words as to what happened after my maid of honour left the palace. The column was met half-way between the landing-place and the city by the Kinwun Mingyi. The troops surrounded the palace, and guards were placed outside the gates while the political officer went in.

There, in the little pavilion in the garden, where they had spent so many happy days, the king and queen surrendered. The queen-mother was with them. This was on the 28th of November, 1885.

The next day the general had an audience of the king and queen, who were then surrounded by the ministers. They were informed that they were to be sent to Rangoon, and at once preparations were made for their departure.

One of the ordinary bullock carts with trotting bullocks, used as hackney carriages in the city, was procured, and the king and queen were put therein; other carriages followed with attendants, and, escorted by mounted infantry, the procession started from the palace for the shore. It was late in the afternoon when they started, and the escort lost their way, and wandered nearly out to the Arracan pagoda, so that it was dark when they came to the steamer landing-place.

The streets were crowded with people, who mostly looked on in silence, but every now and then cries of hate broke out against our troops. "It almost broke our hearts," said an official, " to see our king and queen carried away thus in a common hackney carriage, with no respect of honour shown to them."

And now I will let my maid of honour finish her story.

"When it was rumoured through the city, and the rumour fled like a fire, that the king and queen were to be taken away, I went down with my father and mother to a house near the steamer landing to see the queen for the last time.

"It was nearly dark when they came, and a lamp had to be lit. The carriage stopped and the king and queen got out and stood there. They stood as if wondering at what was happening as if not understanding. Near by were the English troops, and far away as you could see, crowded on every place whence they could get a view, were the people.

"The officer signed to the king to walk along the gangway, but the king hesitated and held back. Ah! Thakin, it was hard on him to take his foot from off his kingdom, from off the land that was his.

"And so he hesitated. Then the officer grew impatient and signed again, and the queen went forward and put her hand in that of the king and led him up the way to the steamer as a mother leads her child when it is lost and afraid.

"They went on board the steamer, and my queen was lost to me for ever.

"In a few moments the steamer let go her moorings and stood out in the great river. I watched and watched from the bank and saw her lights go farther away till they were like a row of stars upon the water. At last I could see no more, for the boat went fast down stream, and my eyes were full of tears.

"Thakin, you may say she was not a good queen, he was not a good king, but they were our own. Do you think we can love a foreign master as we loved our king, who was, as it were, part of ourselves?

"Even now, though many years are past, the people cannot believe that they are gone for ever. They believe that they are in hiding somewhere in the mountains, and will return. If you were to take that hope from them, Thakin, that some day they shall be again a nation, you would break their hearts.

"But my queen will never return again, never—

never see again the golden turrets of her palace
and the pleasant faces of her people.   There is only
the great strange sea before her and the memory
of what has been to tear at her heart for ever."

Printed by BALLANTYNE, HANSON & Co.
London & Edinburgh

www.ingramcontent.com/pod-product-compliance
Lightning Source LLC
Chambersburg PA
CBHW060533030726
47498CB00004B/1180